HEAL MY HEART

KAY SHANEE

B. LOVE PUBLICATIONS

ABOUT THE AUTHOR

Kay is a forty-something wife and mother, born and raised in the Midwest. During the day, she is a high school teacher and track coach. In her free time, she enjoys spending time with her family and friends. Her favorite pastime is reading and writing romance novels about the DOPENESS of BLACK LOVE.

SYNOPSIS

The chemistry between Jaelynn Waters and Kamden Ross could cause an explosion, however, Jaelynn had some healing to tend to, deeming her emotionally unavailable for an all-consuming man like Kamden. Mending her heart takes longer than expected. She's ready to confess her love but it appears that Kamden is no longer in a place to receive it.

Kamden knew Jaelynn was made for him. Still, he gave her the space she required, accepting her as the best friend she was becoming. But after almost two years, Kamden was losing hope in what could be their fortified future. In order to protect his own heart, he thought it was necessary to explore love outside of their defined lines.

Will Kamden finally let go of what could be? Is Jaelynn destined to continue breaking her own heart? Or will love flex its powers and heal what was once broken?

This book is the third book of a spin-off of series that includes "Since the Day We Met" and "Easy To Love." Although the stories can be read separately, you may have a more pleasurable reading experience if you read the aforementioned books.

PREFACE

Warning!!!

This book touches on rape, miscarriage, and assault. If any of this is a trigger for you, you may want to reconsider reading. If you are dealing with any of these issues, please seek help.

Heal My Heart Playlist is Available on Spotify!

*J*aelynn Waters

BEING BACK in Belize was a dream. I'd arrived yesterday morning, along with the rest of the wedding party. I hadn't had much time to relax, because there was so much to do. It didn't matter to me, though; just being here was enough.

A year and a half had passed since I was last here... since I first laid eyes on *him*. Back then, Myla and I were playing matchmaker, reuniting my sister, Braelynn, with her soon-to-be husband, Kyree. While we were here, Myla messed around and ended three years of celibacy with Kyree's younger brother, Kolby, and wound up pregnant with twins. Soon after, they were engaged as well.

Maybe, had I not been afraid, this could be a triple wedding instead of a double. *I don't know what it is about those Ross brothers, but they are, indeed, the whole shebang.* I guess there was no need to dwell on what could have been. Especially since I was finally ready to bare my soul to him and let him know that I was ready to be his.

Everyone was in place, and the instrumental version of "Spend My Life With You" by Eric Benét and Tamia began. The wedding party started their slow walk down the aisle. Kyree and Kolby's parents went first, followed by the mothers of the brides, each holding one of Myla and Kolby's twins, KJ and Mykha. Braelynn and Myla had chosen two cousins each to be bridesmaids. They proceeded down the aisle, alongside Kyree and Kolby's cousins as groomsmen. The only kids that were allowed at the wedding were the twins, and they were only ten months old. So there was no flower girl or ring bearer.

Kamden was the best man, the youngest of the Ross brothers. As I made my way down the aisle, our eyes connected, and I couldn't help but smile. He looked so handsome, standing proudly next to his brothers, with his deep waves, even more pronounced with his fresh Caesar cut, caramel-colored skin, almond-shaped eyes, and kissable lips wrapped in a newly grown goatee. His gaze followed me until I took my place as maid of honor.

Whenever we were in the same room, I felt a supernatural pull on my being. The first time we saw each other in person, I didn't understand what was going on. I didn't want to be attracted to him, but my brain and body were like, *bitch, stop fighting it.* I didn't listen to either, and I'd been fighting for the last year and a half.

The song changed for the entrance of the brides. When the first few notes of "With You" by Tony Terry played, the guests all stood to wait for the brides. I couldn't see them until they were almost in the front. Braelynn was escorted by our uncle, David, and Myla was escorted by her older brother, Myles. More tears were shed by Uncle David and Myles than the two brides. It was so beautiful and very touching.

During the entire ceremony, I couldn't take my eyes off Kamden. I could have been imagining it, but his were on me the whole time as well. I could honestly say that I didn't hear a word that was said by the officiating minister until he announced, "You may now kiss your brides."

I snapped out of my daze and focused on the brides and grooms as they sealed their unions with a kiss. When I looked back at Kamden, his eyes were still on me. As the brides and grooms faced the guests and were pronounced husband and wife, the guests cheered and clapped.

"So Into You" by Tamia began to play, and everyone made their way down the aisle, in reverse order, behind the brides and grooms. Kamden and I met in the middle, and he put his elbow out for me to loop my arm around. I did so, and then he leaned in and kissed my cheek. The electricity that shot through my body caused me to pause for a moment. When he began walking, I shook it off and matched my steps with his.

The receiving line didn't allow for much conversing, but once that was over, we were able to greet each other as we posed what seemed like a million pictures.

"You look beautiful, Jae. I've never seen you with your hair straightened."

I always felt beautiful, but for some reason, when I straightened my hair, I felt it even more. With this heat, it wouldn't be straight for long, though. The wedding colors were lavender and peach, which I thought was a strange combination but looked beautiful together. I wore a peach, off-the-shoulder, fitted dress made with a light, airy material.

"Thank you. I don't straighten it very often. It's a lot of work. You look handsome... as usual."

The men wore traditional black suits. As the best man, Kamden's bow tie was peach, to match my dress, while the groomsmen wore lavender bow ties to match the bridesmaids' dresses.

"I do clean up well. If I do say so myself." He smiled and tugged at his bowtie.

Rolling my eyes, I gently pushed his shoulder. "Arrogant ass."

He shrugged his shoulders.

"What's been up with you?" I asked. "I haven't talked to you in a while."

"I've been returning your texts."

"I know, but they've been dry as hell, and we normally talk on the phone or FaceTime every day. Work keeping you busy?"

"Something like that. You been good, though?" he asked, changing the subject.

I detected something in his demeanor change just then, like he was hiding something. Kamden and I had become very close friends, and I knew him well.

"Yeah. Just busy with the boutique and doing what I can to help them get ready for today."

"I feel you. Looks like we're done here. Let's head to the reception area."

He extended his hand for me to take, and we followed the rest of the wedding party to the area that was designated for the reception. As we lined up to be introduced, I straightened his bow tie, and he used his finger to put some of my hair behind my ear. His hand lingered on my cheek as our eyes connected. His eyes were communicating something to me, but for some reason, I couldn't read them.

"You good?" I asked.

He simply nodded and leaned in to kiss my forehead and then my nose. *One day, he will kiss my lips.* He'd been leaving kisses on my forehead and nose since our friendship began. I was ready for him to kiss my lips.

Each couple had their own entrance song, and Kamden and I chose "Drogba (Joanna)" by Afro B. When I heard the first few beats of the song, I rotated my hips and popped my ass as I took small steps in the direction of our seats. Kamden got behind me and did what guys do when a woman grinds against him. The guests loved it, and the wedding coordinator ate it up.

She said, "Whew! Did the temperature in here just go up twenty degrees or what? These two are hot together!"

It took a few minutes for everyone to quiet down after us. Once they did, "International Players Anthem (I Choose You)" by UGK featuring OutKast blared through the speakers. The brides and grooms were introduced, and we all stood and welcomed them with cheers, shouts, and applause. Kyree and Kolby serenaded their wives as they rapped along with the lyrics. Braelynn and Myla had a cute routine they performed, and I swear, if I wasn't so happy for them and didn't love them so much, I'd be jealous.

As we waited for our food to be served, I decided that now would be a great time to talk to Kamden. It took a long time, but I was finally ready to explore what could happen between us. Our chemistry and attraction had always been undeniable, but I was in no condition to pursue a relationship when we first met. I still had some things I needed to deal with, but fighting my feelings had become exhausting.

"Kam, I've been wanting to talk to you about something."

He gave me his attention. "Oh yeah? Wassup?"

I took a deep breath as my hands began to sweat. I used the tablecloth to dry them off.

"I, umm, I wanted to talk about us."

"What about us?"

"Well, it's been—"

"Hey, baby."

We both turned our heads in the direction of the woman's voice.

Baby?

"Hey, V. You good?" Kamden responded.

"Yeah. The people at my table are cool, but I wanna be with you. Can you come sit with me when you get your food?"

"Of course. This is Jaelynn. Jaelynn, this is my girl, Vida."

His girl? Did he say his girl? Since when did he have a girl? Oh my God, I want to die.

"Hi, Jaelynn. It's nice to finally meet you. He talks about you all the time," Vida said, offering her hand for me to shake.

"Oh really? He hasn't mentioned you at all," I replied, ignoring her hand.

"Yeah. He says your like the sister he's never had. It's good to put a face with the name. Baby, I'll see you in a few." She leaned in to kiss his lips, and her eyes stayed on me. I promise, I almost threw up.

When she walked away, I couldn't even look at Kamden. *Sister he's never had? Wow!* I'd lost my appetite, and all I wanted to do was go to my room and cry until I had no more tears to cry. I couldn't do that, though. It was my sisters' wedding day. I couldn't make this about me.

"I, umm—"

"Your girl, huh?" I interrupted.

"Yeah. I, umm, it's not that serious, but we've been kickin' it for a couple of months."

"Really? Wow. I guess I know why you've been so busy. You have a... girl."

"Jae, I'm—"

"I need to use the bathroom."

I shot up out of my seat quickly and took off to the nearest restroom. I needed a minute to get myself together. Thankfully, it was a single bathroom, and it was empty. I locked the door and leaned up against it.

"God, why did I wait so long?" I asked aloud. "Now, it's too late."

Kamden Ross

Before I could stop her, Jaelynn was gone. She didn't wait for me to apologize or explain. Why I felt the need to do either was beyond me, but I did. So, of course, I went after her and saw her slip into the women's restroom. I pushed on the door, but it was locked.

"Jae, open the door."

"Kamden, I'm using the bathroom. I'll be out in a second."

"Are you okay?"

"Why wouldn't I be?" she snapped.

"Because... I just thought maybe—"

"Kamden, I'm okay. Go enjoy your meal with *your girl*."

Why do I feel like shit? Jaelynn and I keeping shit friendly between us was *her* idea. I simply agreed with what *she* wanted. We clashed when we met, but the attraction was undeniable. It still was. In the midst of my brothers falling in love with her sister and best friend, Jaelynn and I got real close. I'd never stopped wanting her in a romantic way, but I didn't press her, as long as she was a part of my life. After a year and a half of being in the friend zone, I was starting to lose hope of us being anything more.

As friends, Jaelynn and I talked about everything, except our love life. She never mentioned anything about dating at all but would occasionally make comments about the women she assumed I kept in rotation. She was right, but they meant absolutely nothing to me. A nigga just needed to bust a nut every now and then. I probably should have told her about Vida before today, but something kept me from doing so.

Vida was the first woman that I'd dated, that was a little more than just a nut, since I'd met Jaelynn. To me, this was different, which was probably why I didn't mention it. I hadn't planned on bringing Vida on this trip, although I didn't have a problem with her being there. I didn't think we were quite at that stage of our relationship where we traveled together yet. She invited herself and paid her own airfare.

"I'll wait for you. I just wanna make sure you're good."

"Kamden, please. Can you just go? I promise I'm okay."

"Fine," I said, but I didn't leave, not right away.

For a few minutes, I leaned against the bathroom door. I listened for a flushing toilet or water running and heard neither. Instead, I heard her sniffling, and then the sniffling turned into crying, which then turned into sobs.

I didn't know what to do. *Was she crying over me, or was there something else wrong?* After a few more minutes, she had calmed down, and I went back to the reception. Grabbing my food, I went to sit with Vida but couldn't keep my eyes off the main table, waiting for Jaelynn to come back. My mood was shot, and Vida noticed.

"Baby, what's wrong?" she asked.

"Hmm? Oh, I'm good. It's just been a long day."

"Are you gonna be too tired for me to ride your dick tonight?"

"I'll never be too tired for that." I kissed her cheek.

Not long after, the wedding coordinator could be heard on the mic, summoning the best man and maid of honor.

"I'll be back."

By the time I reached the podium, Jaelynn was already there. She gave me a smile that didn't reach her eyes before she began her speech.

"I'll try not to get too emotional. There's so much that I want to say, but we would be here all night. To my sisters, one by blood and one by choice, both of you have been amazing examples for me, in life and in love. Even though the path to get you here, with the men that you love, wasn't always easy, you didn't give up. I admire the way you both followed your hearts and didn't allow the hurt from past relationships to stop you from finding and claiming your true love."

Her eyes connected with mine as she spoke the last part. *I admire the way you both followed your hearts and didn't allow the hurt from past relationships to stop you from finding and claiming your true love.* It felt as if she was speaking directly to my heart.

Was Jaelynn hurt in a past relationship? Is that why she won't give me a chance?

"To my brothers... I didn't know men like you existed in my generation. Thank you for loving my sisters more than you love yourselves. Thank you for setting the standard for what I need to look for in my future husband. I wish you all nothing but love and happiness until the end of time. I love you all."

Again, our eyes met as she spoke about her future husband. It felt like we were the only ones present and she was speaking directly to me. The guests gave her some applause when she ended her speech. She handed me the mic before going to hug her sisters and my brothers. *How in the hell was I going to follow that?*

Once the guests settled down, I cleared my throat and faced my brothers and newly acquired sisters. When I noticed Jaelynn's chair was empty, I searched for her in the crowd and saw her walking away from the reception area. The further away she got, the emptier I felt in inside.

As disappointed as I was, I gave my best man's speech. Although I had no recollection of what I said, I knew it wasn't nearly as touching as Jaelynn's speech. I just wanted it to be over so that I could go find her.

Whatever I said must have been commendable because I got some applause. After hugging Braelynn and Myla, I went to my brothers, who were both standing. We embraced, and when we pulled away, they both gave me a look.

"What?" I asked.

"Don't go after her," Kolby said.

"Did you forget that Vida is here?" Kyree asked.

I closed my eyes and shook my head. *Damn!* I had forgotten all about Vida.

"I just need a few minutes to talk to her."

"Not now you don't. We saw the way y'all were looking at each other. Now isn't the time to do this. Not when you have a whole ass girl." Kyree warned.

"I told you not to bring her. But since you did, go back to your girl. Find another time to talk to Jae, but not now." Kolby added.

I went back to my table to a smiling Vida. She was oblivious to the turmoil that I had going on inside.

"Your speech was great, baby," she said when I sat down.

"Thank you."

I never got a chance to talk to Jaelynn alone because she avoided me for the rest of our stay in Belize, and Vida was on my ass like white on rice. I sent her a few texts, asking her to meet me somewhere, and she replied with a "no" each time.

By the time I got on the flight to head home, I was exhausted from all the pretending I did. Pretending to have a good time, pretending that I wasn't about to blow a damn gasket watching other men flirt with her, pretending to enjoy Vida's company, and pretending that the cold shoulder that Jaelynn gave me didn't bother me. *But what else could a nigga do?*

JAELYNN

One and Half Months Later
New Year's Eve

Things between Kamden and I were different. When I found out that he had been dating someone, I realized that things had been different for a while. He'd been distancing himself from me, and I hadn't realized how much until I met Vida.

My heart shattered when he introduced her as his girl. I wasn't surprised that he followed me to the bathroom; I actually expected it. It angered me when he stood outside the door, asking me if I was okay, though. *Did he really not know how I felt about him?* That question was on repeat in my mind as I got myself together before heading back out to the reception. I got my answer when I ran into Ms. Stella.

"Sweetheart, have you been crying? What's wrong?" she asked.

I thought I'd cleaned up my face pretty well, but I guess not since she could tell that something was wrong.

"I'm okay, Ms. Stella."

"It doesn't look that way to me. Walk with me and tell me the problem."

We began walking slowly toward the area where the reception was being held. Considering my problem had to do with her son, I wasn't sure if she was who I should be talking to.

"You love him, don't you?" Ms. Stella asked.

"Umm..."

"Why are you torturing yourself? Tell him."

"I had some things I needed to sort out, and I didn't want to ruin our friendship by rushing into a relationship, knowing I wasn't ready."

"Are you ready now?"

"I don't know, but not being with him is killing me. I planned to tell him tonight, but I'm not sure my feelings will be reciprocated. Clearly, he's moved on."

"Sweetheart, that chile is just something for him to pass the time. If you tell him how you feel, he will drop that girl in a heartbeat. You've had his heart for a long time."

We stopped walking and faced each other. I was on the verge of another round of tears, but somehow, I kept it together.

"Out of my three boys, Kamden is the most passionate. When he makes up his mind about something, no matter what it is, he puts his all into it. It's been hard for him not to act on his feelings for you, but he respects your decision to just be friends. When you confess to him that you're in love with him, be prepared."

"Be prepared for what?"

"For a love so extraordinarily intense that it may sometimes overwhelm you. He loves with intention, and he loves hard. Make sure you're ready."

She left me standing there in my thoughts, but I had no time to process it all because they were calling for the maid of honor and best man speech.

I'd forgotten about my talk with Ms. Stella, until now. Kamden and I were worse off than we were then. Since we got over the clashing of our personalities from when we first met, there was a point when we communicated in some way every day. Sometimes it was by text, sometimes by a phone call, but most times, it was through FaceTime. Often, it was all three. At first, it was weird because our attraction to each other was so obvious. However, he respected my wishes about keeping things on the friendship level and easily became one of my best friends.

I was the first person he told about wanting to start his own business. He was the first person I told about wanting to start an online men's sleepwear store. When he told me that he wanted four to six kids, all by the time he turned thirty-five, I thought he was kidding, but he was serious as a heart attack. At the time, he was twenty-six and single with no prospects. Even though that sounded crazy to me, I was still crushing on him hard. I truly missed the way we once were.

I'd pretty much stopped initiating communication with Kamden. After our siblings' wedding, I came home and threw myself into work. MyLynn's Bedroom Boutique was thriving because I used work as a distraction. Kamden reached out to me about a week after we returned from Belize. I wasn't sure what he was looking for, but I was certain he didn't find it.

"Hey," I said when I answered his FaceTime call.

"Wassup? How you been?"

"Good. Just working."

We stared at each other quietly for an uncomfortable amount of time before he spoke again.

"Jae, are we good?"

I cleared my throat and looked away from him.

"Naw, look at me. I need to see those eyes," he said.

"We're good, Kam."

"At the wedding, you wanted to talk about us. What about us?"

I released a chuckle and rolled my eyes. Over a week had passed since I started that conversation. Whatever I wanted to say then was irrelevant now.

"It's not important."

"Why would you say that? Anything you have to say is important, Jae. Outside of my brothers, you're my best friend."

"Or like the sister you've never had?"

That comment must have caught him by surprise because he didn't have a response.

"Exactly! Kam, you're in a relationship, and I understand that's gonna change the dynamic of us. It's cool. I'm good."

"It doesn't have to change, Jae."

"It already has."

"That's because of work. I've just been busy with work." *He lied.*

"Okay, Kam."

"So we good?"

"We're good. I gotta go. I'll call you later." *I lied.*

I ended that call and cried for hours afterward. I wanted to tell him my true feelings for him and why it had taken me so long to give in to them, but I didn't think it mattered anymore. From that point on, if he reached out to me, I responded, but I kept the conversation short and light. It was rare that I'd contact him first.

A few days ago, I was excited when he told me that he still planned to come to Seattle for New Year's Eve. It was something we'd talked about, but I wasn't sure if that was still his plan since he had a girlfriend. It would be the second time that we'd celebrated the holiday together. However, my excitement quickly dissipated when he told me that said girlfriend, Vida, was coming as well. That bit of news had soured my mood for the days that followed.

I couldn't even call Braelynn and Myla to complain, because I hadn't shared with them my feelings for Kamden. Everyone knew that we had a mutual attraction for each other, but nobody knew that I was in love with him.

Tonight, I had to put on a happy face because Kamden and Vida would be arriving at the club in a matter of minutes. To stop myself from looking at the VIP entrance every five seconds, I went to the bathroom that was in the back of the VIP area.

"I'll be right back, Nae. I'm going to the bathroom."

"Okay."

Nae, or Danae, was someone I went to high school with. We weren't the best of friends, but we got along well. She wasn't someone I shared any of my secrets or personal business with; I had Braelynn and Myla for that. But she was cool to hang out with. Since my sisters moved to Chicago, Nae and I had been hanging out a little more.

In the bathroom, I took in my appearance. My thin frame was wrapped in a fitted, silver, sequined romper. Turning around, I admired the way the romper fit my small but plump ass. On my feet, I wore a pair of black booties. My legs were bare and smooth to the touch. *Too bad no one would be touching them tonight.* I'd gotten my hair straightened again, and it hung to the middle of my back with a part on the side and some loose curls throughout. I looked amazing. Alone, but amazing, nonetheless.

As I reentered the VIP section, I saw Kamden and Vida standing near the stairs. Kamden was looking around, and when he spotted me, a huge smile graced his face before he made his way toward me.

"Jae," he said as he wrapped his arms around my waist and lifted me from the floor. "Damn, baby girl. I missed you."

I hugged him back and inhaled his scent, almost forgetting where we were and who we were to each other. He put me down and took a step back, eyes roaming over my body.

"You're beautiful," he said.

"Thank you. You look good, too."

Behind him, Vida cleared her throat. He turned around and said, "Oh, Vida. You remember Jaelynn."

"Of course," she said with a smile that wasn't really a smile. "How have you been?"

"Good. Umm, so we have this whole area. Danae's uncle owns the place, so he hooked us up. There's champagne, Grey Goose, Hennessy, and some other stuff on the tables. Help yourself."

I turned my ass around and went back to sit next to Danae. She'd met Kamden last year when he came for New Year's Eve. Getting her to believe there was nothing going on between us was damn near impossible. She thought I was crazy for friend-zoning him because she saw the chemistry between us.

"Who the hell is that bitch with Kamden?" Danae asked as soon as my ass hit the seat.

"Nae! Don't do that. You don't even know that woman, and she ain't done nothing to you. That's Kam's girlfriend."

"The fuck? Why is he wasting his time when he knows damn well he's in love with you? Stevie Wonder can see that shit."

"Shut up, Nae. Here they come."

"Danae, it's good to see you again. This is Vida. Vida, this is one of Jaelynn's friends, Danae."

Vida stuck her hand out, and Danae made herself seem busy so she wouldn't have to shake her hand.

"Nice to meet you," Vida said, pulling her hand back.

Danae didn't return the sentiment, and I nudged her. She looked at me and rolled her eyes, still not speaking. Danae and I weren't besties, but she was good people, and I knew she was on my team.

"Help yourself to the drinks. The food should be coming up in a little while," Danae said, almost dismissively.

Kamden gave me a questioning look, and I shrugged my shoulders. He ended up sitting next to me with Vida on his other side. He poured her a drink, then himself, and they talked amongst themselves for a little while.

"Jaelynn, I wanted to tell you that I love your lingerie line. I ordered a few pieces and... let me just say, they did exactly what they were supposed to do and more," Vida said, eyeing Kamden and looking extremely satisfied.

Kamden, on the other hand, shifted uncomfortably in his seat. When I looked at him, he avoided my eyes and took a sip of his drink.

"Oh, that's great, Vida. It's always nice to hear good things from customers."

"My friends have ordered some items as well. They were very pleased. Let me know if you need someone to promote on Instagram. I would definitely do it for some free items."

"Oh, okay. I'll run the idea by my sisters." I lied.

"Why are you lying to that girl?" Danae whispered.

I shrugged my shoulders. There was no way I was about to let the woman who ruined my life represent my company. I'd kill myself first.

"How have you been, Jae? Business still good?" Kamden asked.

"I've been fine, and business is still good. How about you?"

"I've been okay. Business is going well. I secured a few more contracts, so I had to add a few more people to my crew."

Kamden had recently earned a degree in business. While he was in school, he worked maintenance with his father. He started his own cleaning and janitorial company about a year ago.

"That's great, Kam. I'm so proud of you."

He smiled. "Thank you. I'm proud of you, too."

The food had finally arrived, and the waitresses placed the trays on the long table that sat in the back of VIP. Most of the people in the area with us were Danae's family and some of their friends. Once the food arrived, everyone migrated in that direction.

"I'll go get us some food," Vida offered Kamden before kissing his cheek and leaving.

Danae had gone to get food as well, leaving Kamden and I alone. We listened to the music, bobbing our heads to the old-school song by Musiq Soulchild, "Just Friends". *Ironic, huh?* There was a nervous energy between us.

"You're not hungry?" Kamden asked.

"I'll get something in a bit."

"I can get it for you," he offered.

I shook my head. "What kind of sense would it make for you to go get food for me when your girlfriend is getting food for you and her?"

He nodded and smiled. "Yeah, I guess that wouldn't make any sense."

There was some activity near the stairs, where the entrance to VIP was located, and I looked in that direction. When I saw who it was, my heart almost stopped.

"What the fuck is he doing here?" I unknowingly said aloud.

"Who is he?" Kamden asked.

"My ex."

I watched as my ex, Drake, his younger brother Drew, and three of their rowdy ass friends entered the area. I closed my eyes and wished that I could disappear. My right leg, the leg closest to Kamden, began to shake. When I felt a hand on my knee, I opened my eyes and looked at Kamden.

"What's wrong?" he asked.

"Huh? Uhh, nothing. I'm—I'm good." I nodded nervously.

"Why are you shaking?"

"I didn't know I was. I'm gonna go grab some food."

Before he could say anything else, I was up and headed toward the food. Unfortunately, Drake saw me and grabbed me by the arm, then pulled me into his chest. His hands went around my waist, and he pressed his body against mine.

"Jaebaby," he said, using the nickname he'd given me. Hearing it made me nauseous.

Putting both hands against his chest, I struggled to push away from him.

"Let me go, Drake!"

"Come on, Jaebaby. Don't be like that. You know you the only girl I ever loved."

"Drake, please. Let me go."

He released me, and I punched him in the chest.

"Keep your fuckin' hands off me!"

I marched away, and instead of going to get food, I went to the bathroom. Once inside, I locked the door and slowly counted to ten, trying to keep myself from having a panic attack. I'd managed to avoid seeing Drake for almost two years. *Why now? Why tonight?*

A knock on the door scared the shit out of me, and I moved to the wall on the other side.

"Jae, it's me," Kamden said. "Open the door."

"No, Kam. I'll be out in a second."

"Jae, don't make me cause a scene. Open this damn door."

Taking a few deep breaths, I opened the door.

"What's up with you and dude?" he asked as soon as he entered, closing the door behind him.

"Nothing. He's my ex, and he still tries to holla. That's it."

"Why the fuck you get so nervous when you saw him?"

"Kam, we haven't been together in two years. He just annoys me, okay? Leave it alone."

I pushed past him and left him in the bathroom. I'd lost what little appetite I had, so I went back to my seat. Vida and Danae were back and enjoying the food. I took my phone out and looked at the time. *Fifteen minutes until midnight.*

Kamden slid between Vida and I, giving me a look of concern. "You're not gonna eat, Jae?" he asked.

"No. I'm fine."

I looked around the room at everyone enjoying themselves. If I could just make it to 12:15, I could fake a headache and go home. *You can make it thirty minutes, Jae.* I gave myself a pep talk.

As it neared midnight, the music and crowd got hype. The DJ was playing "How Do You Want It" by Teyana Taylor ft. King Combs. I didn't want to be near Kamden and his girl when they rang in the new year with a kiss, so I poured myself a glass of champagne and told Danae I was gonna get a view of the crowd.

The DJ gave us the two-minute before midnight warning and continued to hype us up. I felt a presence behind me, and my body cringed, letting me know that it was Drake. I put my glass of champagne on the ledge and took a couple of steps to the side, turning to face him.

"Drake—"

"I come in peace." He cut me off, putting his hands up.

Neither of us spoke for a minute.

"Why are you bothering me, Drake?"

"It's been a while. I just wanted to see how you doing?"

"Like you give a fuck!"

"I do!"

"After what you did to me?"

"Jaebaby, you know I ain't mean no harm. I would never hurt you, intentionally."

"Fuck you, Drake."

When I tried to walk away, he blocked me and wrapped his arms around my waist.

"Drake—"

His lips landed on mine as my hands went to his chest. I wasn't strong enough to get away from him, so I brought my knee to his nuts as hard as I could. He released me and bent over, groaning in pain. Kamden was at my side as I backed away from Drake.

"Jae, what the fuck?" he said.

"I gotta go!"

I ran down the stairs and maneuvered my way through the club. When I made it to the door, I felt someone's hand on my shoulder. I turned around and saw Kamden's worried face.

"I can't let you leave like this, Jae. Not alone. It's late, and—"

"Don't worry about me. Just make sure he doesn't come after me."

I pushed through security and the doors before Kamden could

stop me. When I got outside, I realized that I didn't have my coat, and it was forty degrees. *My dumb ass!* Pulling out my phone, I went to the Uber app and saw that there was one three minutes away. I couldn't wait to get home and forget this day ever happened.

KAMDEN

Over the past couple of months, things between Jaelynn and I had changed. Every conversation we'd had since returning from Belize, whether by call or text, was initiated by me. Regardless of how I attempted to engage her in conversation, her responses were always short and to the point. She stopped answering my FaceTime calls, so when I saw her today, it was the first time I'd seen her in over two months.

My work schedule was only part of the reason that things between Jaelynn and I were different. Vida was the other part—well, my relationship with her. Vida hadn't been an issue at all. She didn't seem overly concerned about how close Jaelynn and I were... or how close we used to be, because we were definitely drifting apart.

When Vida and I arrived, I looked around for Jaelynn but didn't see her at first. A minute or so later, she came from the back area, and *damn*, did she look amazing. Her dainty frame in the shiny silver romper had my dick jumping. The vibe between Jaelynn and I tonight felt good, but the minute her ex entered VIP, something about her demeanor changed, and not in a good way. Although she said it was nothing, I knew that was some bullshit.

I kept my eyes on her, as she stood a few feet away, overlooking the crowd below. I watched as her body tensed when her ex approached her from behind. She turned to face him, and they exchanged a few words that I could tell weren't pleasant based on her mannerisms.

"Baby, it's almost time," Vida said, taking my attention away from Jaelynn and her ex.

"Five... Four... Three... Two... One! Happy New Year!"

The entire place erupted, and Vida pulled my face to hers for a kiss. When she released me, I looked toward Jaelynn, and she looked to be struggling to get away from her ex. By the time I got to her, she had kneed him in his nuts, and he was on the floor.

"Jae, what the fuck?"

"I gotta go!" she said, before taking off down the stairs.

Without hesitating, I went after her and was able to grab her shoulder before she went out the door.

"I can't let you leave like this, Jae. Not alone. It's late, and—"

"Don't worry about me. Just make sure he doesn't come after me."

She pushed through security and was outside before I could stop her again. Pissed off, I went back up to VIP to find her ex. I definitely needed to have a word with the nigga. When I made it up the stairs, my eyes scanned the area. I spotted him in the corner talking to the dudes he came in with. I made a beeline toward him, and Danae and Vida hopped in front of me.

"Baby, let's just go," Vida suggested.

"Kamden, Drake is ignorant as hell. Him and his boys always on some dumb shit, and I don't want you to get caught up." Danae added.

As much as I wanted to confront the nigga, Danae was right. This wasn't my city, and I didn't have my brothers with me. I was outnumbered, and I wasn't dumb enough to start some shit I couldn't finish. Nodding, I headed back to where we were seated. After helping Vida with her coat, we said goodbye Danae.

"Jae left her coat. I can take it to her if—" She began.

"Naw, I got it. Thanks."

Once Vida and I were in an Uber and headed for our hotel, she asked, "Is Jaelynn okay?"

"Physically? Yeah, she's good. I'm not sure what the deal is between her and her ex, but I plan to find out."

"He probably just wants her back. I don't think you need to get involved."

Before I could catch myself, the words, "I didn't ask what you thought," spilled out of my mouth.

She leaned back and snatched her arm from around mine. "Excuse the hell outta me! What she has going on with her ex is their business. Why would you get mixed up in it?"

I didn't respond, because it wasn't necessary. No more words were spoken until we pulled up in front of the hotel. I got out, tapped on the driver's window, and waited for him to let it down.

"Can you wait for me here? I need to make another stop."

He nodded.

I walked around to the other side and helped Vida out. On the way to our room, I could sense that she had an attitude, but I couldn't concern myself with that. My mind was on Jaelynn and making sure she was good.

"Do you have your key?" I asked.

Instead of replying, she reached in her little purse to retrieve it. She let us inside the room, and I looked around to make sure everything was good.

"I'll be back. I'm going to check on Jae."

"Seriously, Kamden? It's New Year's Eve. Our night has already been partially ruined. You trying to fuck up the whole thing?"

"I need you to be a little more understanding. If I stay here, my mood is gon' be fucked up because I'm worried about my friend.

Let me make sure she's good, and when I come back, I can focus on you."

"I might have been born at night, but it wasn't last night, nigga. If you leave, don't expect me to still be here when you get back." She threatened.

"You want me to choose between you and Jae?"

She put all her weight on one leg, folded her arms across her chest, and cocked her head to the side.

"Look, if you're still here when I get back, we can talk. If not, it's been real."

"Are you serious?"

"As a heart attack. And don't be stupid and fuck up my shit if you decide to leave."

Anything else she had to say, she said it to my back.

On the way to Jaelynn's house, I replayed the events of the night in my head. Vida could be right about her ex wanting her back. But something about Jaelynn's reaction when she saw him didn't sit well with me. There was more to story, and I was determined to find out.

JAELYNN

*W*hen I got home, I sent out a group text to tell everyone Happy New Year and that I was home safe and going to bed. After peeling out of my romper, I threw on a T-shirt and put my hair up in a bun. In my bathroom, I washed the makeup off my face, then went to the kitchen. I grabbed the carton of strawberry ice cream from the freezer. Not even bothering to get a bowl, I got a spoon out of the drawer and dug in.

"Yummm," I moaned.

As I enjoyed the ice cream, I thought about the last time I'd seen Drake almost two years ago. We'd been broken up for a couple of months, and I'd blocked him from contacting me in any way. Unfortunately, we ended up at the same event for a mutual friend. Myla had come with me because Braelynn was with her ex, Samuel. She'd spotted him first, and we tried to avoid him to no avail.

"Jaebaby, how you been?"

"Fuck you, Drake."

I rolled my eyes and tried to walk past him, but he gripped my arm tightly and held me in place. With his mouth right next to my ear, he whispered, "You know that pussy is still mine, right? Don't get nobody fucked up while you here."

He loosened his hold, and I yanked my arm away. "This pussy will never be yours again. Stay the fuck away from me."

Myla and I walked away, and I was on edge for the rest of the night. She did her best to get my mind off my run-in with Drake, but nothing seemed to help. We ended up leaving sooner than we planned.

When I made it home, after dropping Myla off, Drake was parked in front of my house. Exhaling deeply, I got out of my car and went to my front door. Drake was right behind me. Turning around, I leaned against the screen door and waited for Drake to say what he needed to say.

"Why you gotta look so irritated to see me? You hate me that much?"

"I do, Drake. I hate you that much."

"I apologized to you a hundred times. Shit ain't been right since you stop fuckin' with me. Tell me what I need to do to get you back."

"There's nothing you can do, Drake. We're done, and ain't no turning back. Have a good night."

I turned around and opened the screen door, then unlocked the front door. When I stepped inside, I immediately pushed the door to close it in Drake's face, but he stopped it with his foot.

"Drake, move!"

He shoved the door open, causing me to take a step back to avoid getting hit.

"What the fuck? Just leave, Drake. There's nothing else to say."

He closed and locked the door before turning to face me.

"That's cool. I ain't wanna talk anyway."

Until then, I'd never feared Drake. Something about the tone of his voice and the look in his eyes triggered my fight-or-flight senses. My eyes scanned the living room for an object that I could use as a weapon.

"I'm not here to hurt you, Jaebaby. You the only girl I ever loved."

"Then what do you want? Why are you here?"

"Because I still love you, and I just want things to be the way they used to be."

He moved toward me, and I moved back until he had me trapped against the wall. I turned my head to the left so my face wouldn't be in his chest.

"Don't you miss how things used to be?" he whispered.

He grabbed my chin and turned my face, before lifting it to his. When he bent his head to kiss me, I pressed my lips together and moved my head from side to side.

"You gon' make this shit worse than it needs to be, Jaebaby." He warned.

An alarm suddenly went off in my head, and I just went crazy. My arms were swinging, my legs were kicking, and I was screaming as loud as I could. Drake put his hand over my mouth to shut me up and pinned me back against the wall.

"I told your hardheaded ass I wasn't gon' hurt you. Shut the fuck up before I change my mind."

His hand covered my mouth as we stared each other down. My chest heaved up and down as I tried to calm myself.

"I'm gon' move my hand, but if you scream again, I'm gon' slap the shit outta you."

My eyes got big at his threat. He'd never raised his voice at me, let alone a hand. He uncovered my mouth slowly, then covered my lips with his. The kiss was so soft; I barely felt it.

"I just want to make love."

A frown covered my face as he continued.

"I can't bust a nut with these other bitches. My dick only responds to your pussy. I need you, Jaebaby."

I couldn't believe my ears. There was no way I was fucking this nigga. He must've been out of his damn mind. As much as I wanted to curse his ass out, I remained calm.

"*Drake, I don't want to have sex with you. If you make me, that would be considered rape. Are you gonna rape me?*"

"*It's not rape. You my girl. You gon' always be my fuckin' girl. This pussy...*" he yanked my skirt up and groped me between the legs, "*...gon' always be mine.*"

This nigga is really about to rape me!

The doorbell brought me back to the present. I looked at the ice cream I was eating, and it was starting to melt. After putting it back in the freezer, I wiped my tears and went to the door.

"Who is it?" I asked but assumed it was Danae.

"It's Kam. Open the door."

What is he doing here?

Before turning off the alarm and unlocking the door, I looked through the peephole to see if Vida was with him. I breathed a sigh of relief when I didn't see her.

"Damn, Jae. You didn't want me to come in?" he asked when I finally opened the door.

"What are you doing here? Where's Vida?" I asked, ignoring his question.

He stepped in and turned to lock the door behind him, then secured the alarm. Before moving away from the door, he tossed my coat on the couch, then took off the blazer he was wearing and did the same with it as he had with my coat.

"I came to check on you. Vida's at the hotel."

He followed me to the kitchen, and I leaned against the counter while he stood in the entryway and leaned on the frame.

"I'm fine. You should go back to your girl."

"When did we start lying to each other? I can see you've been crying."

Folding my arms across my chest, I bowed my head and realized that I was only wearing a T-shirt. It was just long enough to cover my ass but not much more.

"Okay, I was upset, but I'm good now. I'm sure Vida wasn't happy when you left her to come check on me."

"Why you keep bringing her up? Have I not made it clear to you that you're my priority?"

He stepped in front of me and dipped his index finger under my chin, lifting my head. Our eyes connected, and he continued when I didn't say anything.

"I know fear when I see it, Jae. What did that nigga do to you?"

Looking away from him, I said, "It was just a bad breakup."

"You can't even look at me and say that. You still lying to me, Jae?"

I faced him again but didn't repeat myself.

"I've known you for almost two years, and you ain't mentioned him once. How long ago was this breakup?"

"Two years ago."

"Why'd you break up?"

Standing so close to him, breathing in his scent, feeling the heat radiating between our bodies, the thin T-shirt I was wearing with no bra and only a thong underneath was all too much. If he glanced down, he'd see my hard nipples through the fabric, and I was willing to bet he could smell my womanly scent because my thong was soaked.

I swallowed, even though my mouth was dry as hell. "Typical nigga shit. I got tired of all his side hoes bringing drama to my doorstep."

"Were you... in love with him?"

I detected something in his voice when he asked that... something that sounded a little like fear.

"I've only ever loved one man... but I waited too long to tell him, and now, he's... unavailable."

His expression changed as if he was trying to decipher the meaning of my words. I looked up at him, waiting for him to respond. At first, I thought I was imagining his lips getting closer to mine, but it wasn't my imagination. I closed my eyes and waited for them to meet.

KAMDEN

*W*hen Jaelynn answered the door in a T-shirt that barely covered her ass, I knew I was in trouble. Yes, I'd seen her in next to nothing before—a bikini, a short dress, a pair of tiny shorts—but we were always around groups of people, so I was able to control my urges.

She walked away and led me into the kitchen, allowing me a chance to adjust my dick. The purpose of my visit was to make sure that she was mentally and emotionally okay. Her mouth continued to say that she was, but her eyes told another story.

I was expecting the reason for their breakup to be something grand, not "typical nigga shit". *If he was cheating on her and she wasn't in love with him, why did seeing him tonight affect her the way it did?* I planned to get the answer to that when she threw my ass for a loop.

"Were you... in love with him?" I asked, admittedly afraid of what her answer would be.

"I've only ever loved one man," she said softly. "But I waited too long to tell him, and now, he's... unavailable."

Her words made me think back to her speech at our sibling's

wedding. Just like then, it felt as if she was speaking to my heart. I leaned in so slowly that I wasn't sure I was moving. She closed her eyes and waited for me to plant my lips on hers, and just before they connected, I heard frantic banging on the front door.

"The fuck?" I said.

Jaelynn was visibly shaken and stayed close behind me, holding on to the back of my shirt, as we went to the front of the house. The banging was nonstop from the first knock, and as I reached to unlock and open the door, I felt Jaelynn tug my shirt.

"It's the middle of the night," she whispered before stepping in front of me and looking though the peephole.

Before she could tell me who it was, the person on the other side of the door added shouting to the pounding.

"Jaebaby! Open the door. I promise not to hurt you."

"Is that—"

"Drake, my ex."

"I just wanna talk. That's all. I swear," Drake pleaded through the door, pounding on it a few more times.

She looked at me with pleading eyes and put her finger in front of her lips, asking me to be quiet.

"I need to see you, Jaebaby. Real shit. I wanna apologize for what happened."

She looked at me, then quickly looked away. *Was he talking about what happened tonight?*

"Jaebaby, come on. I know you hear me. Let me come in and apologize. I was fucked up that night. You know that shit ain't me."

No, some other night.

Jaelynn sat on the arm of the sofa chair, wrapped her arms around her waist, and began rocking back and forth.

"Fuck this shit!" I said, moving to the door.

"Nooo, please, Kam." She hopped between me and the door. "He'll leave," she whispered.

In her eyes, I saw that same fear that I saw at the club. Based on the shit he said from the other side of the door and her behavior, I assumed the worst. But I didn't want to believe where my thoughts were taking me.

I pulled Jaelynn into my chest and wrapped my arms around her. After a few minutes, Drake finally gave up and took his ass on. It was time for Jaelynn to give me some answers.

Once I was seated on the couch, she followed suit but left some space between us. Grabbing the blanket that was thrown across the back of the couch, she extended her legs to the other end, threw the blanket over her legs, then rested her head on my lap. My hands went to her head, and I began to massage her scalp.

"What was that about, Jae?"

For at least five minutes, she said nothing. I thought she may have fallen asleep. When she finally spoke, it was just above a whisper.

"This is hard to say, which is one of the reasons no one knows."

I continued massaging her scalp, not wanting to say anything to disrupt her thoughts.

"We'd been broken up for about two months. Myla and I went to a party, and he was there..."

She went on to tell me the events that occurred that evening. The more she told me, the more pissed off I became. I began to regret not fucking that nigga up when I had the opportunity.

"I didn't expect him to be here when I got home. I should have went back to Myla's house. In a million years, I never would have believed he would do something so terrible."

"What did he do?"

"I told him I didn't want to have sex with him."

My heart stopped.

"I told him if he forced me, it was rape," she cried.

God, please don't let her tell me that this nigga raped her. I think I stopped breathing as she continued.

"He said, 'it's not rape because I'm gon' always be his girl.' He said, 'my pussy was always gon' be his.'"

My whole pants leg was wet from her tears as she relived what was probably the worst night of her life.

"Jae, please... please don't tell me that nigga raped you."

"He yanked my skirt up and ripped my panties off."

I lifted her head and pulled her body next to mine. She buried her face in my chest, allowing me to wrap her in my arms. I knew I had to be strong for her, but I couldn't stop the few tears that fell from my eyes.

"He raped me," she cried into my chest. "He raped me, Kam. Why would he—"

"Shhh... Baby girl, please don't cry. It wasn't your fault." I grabbed her shoulders and pushed her back so I could see her face. "Do you hear me? It wasn't your fault. Weak ass niggas do shit like that. He don't deserve to still be breathing."

Her head went back to my chest, and I comforted her as best I could. She said she hadn't told anyone, which meant she'd been dealing with this shit alone all this time. I'd never been in this kind of situation, but I was already trying to figure out how to make the nigga pay for what he did.

My mind went in ten different directions as I tried to figure out how to help Jaelynn. I didn't know how much time had passed, but I noticed that she was no longer crying. When I looked down at her in my arms, the light from the kitchen allowed me to see that she'd fallen asleep. I sat there for a good while before cradling her in my arms and taking her to her bedroom.

I managed to pull her comforter back with one hand, then gently placed her in the bed. When I released her, her eyes popped open, and she reached for me. Our eyes met, and she didn't say a word, yet I still knew exactly what she was asking.

"I'm not going anywhere." I assured her.

I took my phone out of my pocket and saw that Vida had called and texted me multiple times. Not bothering to read the texts, call her back, or take my phone off silent mode, I put it on Jaelynn's dresser. After undressing down to my boxers, I slid in the bed next to Jaelynn.

Without exchanging any words, she put her head on my chest and threw her arm across my stomach. My arm was draped across her shoulder, and I hugged her tight, kissing the top of her head. After a few minutes of silence, I thought she'd fallen back to sleep until I felt her tears wetting up my chest.

"Jae, I'm here. I'll be here as long as you need me. I gotchu, baby girl."

Eventually, she fell asleep, wrapped in my arms. While she slept, I came up with a plan. He got away with that shit for two years, but his time was up.

JAELYNN

I'd had many dreams about Kamden, but none felt as real as the current one I was having. My hand was in his boxer briefs, stroking his erection. When I heard him grunt, I slid underneath the comforter and pulled his underwear down, just enough to keep his dick exposed.

When my tongue touched the head, I heard him hiss. After licking around the tip a few times, enjoying the taste of his precum, I licked up and down his length. Finally, I took him in my mouth, and his hand went to my head.

"Fuck, Jae."

My head bobbed up and down as I tried to take in as much of him as I could, using my hand for what I couldn't. As saliva seeped from the sides of my mouth, I moaned, and the vibrations must have done something to him.

Suddenly, he snatched me up, and we were face-to-face. He pushed the T-shirt I was wearing up my body and over my head before our lips connected and our tongues collided, wrestling for control. I felt his hand on my ass just before he grabbed the thin string of my thong and ripped it away.

Like they were meant for each other, his dick found the entrance to my slick haven and slid right on in. We both released moans of satisfaction. He tore his mouth away from mine and attacked each of my breasts, one at a time, before he pushed them together and covered both nipples with his tongue. My titties weren't big, so I didn't know how he made that shit work. The slight discomfort that I felt as the width of his manhood stretched me wide was worth it when he hit my spot.

"Ahh, shit!" I screamed.

"Damn, Jae! This pussy is better than I ever dreamed, baby girl."

He had that shit right because his dick was phenomenal. It was so good that I didn't want the dream to end. My hands pressed down on his chest, and I rode his dick until I felt my pussy clench around him. My movements slowed as I tried to extend my climax.

"Fuck, Kam! I love you so much!" I screamed as I rained down on him.

"Damn, Jae! I love your ass, too. Shit, I can't pull out, baby girl."

I felt him throbbing inside of me as he filled me with his seeds. Once his release was complete, he pulled me into a heated kiss. When our lips parted, he wrapped his arms around me, and within seconds, the dream was over.

WHEN I OPENED MY EYES, I was laying on my stomach. It felt as if I was straddling a hard, thick frame. Before I moved, I tried to recollect what happened the night before. I knew damn well I came home alone. I tried to sit up, but it seemed as though I was being restrained.

"You trying to go somewhere?" I heard a voice that sounded eerily like Kamden's say.

Oh shit! Am I... Did we... Wait a minute!

"Kam?"

"Yeah, baby girl?"

My eyes went wide, and I pushed myself up. I looked down at his naked chest, my naked body, and how we were connected.

"Oh my God! That wasn't a dream? That was real?"

"Jae," he said, gripping my hips, and thrusting upward one good time. "My hard dick is still inside you. It was very real, baby girl."

"We shouldn't—"

Somehow, he managed to flip me over, without disengaging our connection. Now on my back, I looked up at Kamden's handsome face.

"Don't even say that shit. Do you know how long I've fantasized about this very moment?"

My head went from left to right.

"Too damn long."

He kissed my lips and began to give me slow, deep strokes. My legs clamped around his waist, and I attempted to match his moves. Kamden released my mouth, only to latch on to my neck. Sucking, biting, then kissing, surely leaving his mark.

"Shit, Kam. I can't—we shouldn't—what about—fuuccckk! I'm cummin'!"

"Good! Wet my shit up while I fill your shit up."

We came simultaneously, and *my goodness!* The feeling sent me beyond the stars. Both of us were breathing hard, yet Kam managed to leave a trail of soft kisses along my neck, then my cheek, before ending at my mouth. He rolled onto his back, and we lost our connection. Right away, I felt a sense of loss.

"C'mere," he said, raising his arm so I could rest my head on his shoulder. "Last night—"

"I don't wanna talk about it."

"Jae, you've been dealing with this shit by yourself for a long time. Have you thought about going to the police?"

"No," I answered quickly, and it was only partially true.

"Maybe—"

"No, I'm not going to the police. I just want to forget about it."

Going to the police crossed my mind a couple of times when it first happened. But I was too afraid and embarrassed, and I felt dumb as hell for letting it happen.

"But you haven't. This ain't something that is easily forgotten, baby girl."

"Going to the police won't help me forget. It's just... seeing him last night triggered some things. If you hadn't been here, I probably would have shot his ass."

"But I was. No need to think about the what-ifs. Wait... you got a gun?"

"I do... and I know how to use it."

"That's good to know." He kissed the top of my head and gave me a squeeze. "What about counseling?"

"What about it?"

"Have you gone?"

"Kam, you are the only person I've talked to about this. I don't like talking about it, and I manage to block it out more times than not. I know it seemed like I was a mess last night, but most of the time, I'm good."

"What about the times when you're not good? How often do you feel paranoid or have nightmares? When was the last time you went on a date or let a man get this close to you?"

I was almost always paranoid. It wasn't as bad when Braelynn moved in with me for a little while after she'd broken up with Samuel. I was happy that she'd found true love with Kyree, but I dreaded the day she moved for good. Being alone again brought back my paranoia. As far as dating and sex, I had absolutely no interest in either until I'd fallen in love with Kamden.

"The paranoia and the nightmares come and go, I don't date, and you're the first man that I've been with since it happened."

I guess he had to let that sink in because he didn't respond for a few minutes. When he did, he said, "Can I ask you something?"

"Sure?"

"How long before Belize did it happen?"

"About two months," I said softly.

"Shit, Jae. Those nightmares you were having—"

"I had nightmares in Belize?" I had no recollection of that.

"You did. A few times, I woke up to you tossing and turning. You were mumbling something that I didn't understand. We didn't know each other that well, and you were so damn mean to me, so I didn't say anything about it. That explains so much about your attitude. I'm sorry for being an asshole."

"Why are you apologizing? I should be the one apologizing. You were just giving back what I put out there. I was such a bitch to you, and I didn't understand why until months later."

"Why were you?"

"After that shit happened, I couldn't imagine ever wanting to be with another man. Just the thought of it took me to a dark place. Then you came along, all fine and raised right and shit. I was so attracted to you, and I didn't want to be... I didn't think I should be. I remembered thinking that if I could think about sex, after that, maybe it wasn't rape. Maybe I encouraged him in some way."

He slid his arm from around me and turned to lay on his side. Our faces were only inches apart.

"Listen to me. What that nigga did was wrong. You told him no, and he forced himself on you. You didn't encourage him, you didn't ask for it, and it wasn't your fault. Do you understand?"

I nodded.

"I need to hear you tell me you understand."

"I understand."

"Look, baby girl, I'm not trying to tell you how to handle this situation. I know you have to deal with it the best way that you can. Promise me you'll think about counseling, though."

"I'll think about it."

He kissed my forehead, my nose, and then... my lips. *Finally, my lips!*

"I have to go." He started. "I told Vida I'd be back hours ago."

Vida... I hadn't forgotten about her, but I had pushed her to the back of my mind. I pulled the comforter up to my neck and turned away from him. He moved closer to me, until my back was against his chest, and slid his arm around my waist.

"Don't do that, Jae. It's not even what you think. She gave me an ultimatum last night. Told me to choose, and you see where I'm at."

"Then why do you have to leave?"

"Damn, Jae. I brought the girl all the way to Seattle. The least I can do is make sure she straight. It's not her fault she got involved with a man whose heart belonged to someone else."

I turned back around to face him with a big, cheesy ass grin on my face.

"Why you smiling? I didn't say my heart belonged to you."

I gasped before sitting up, grabbing a pillow, and swinging it at his head.

"Aye, calm your little ass down." He pulled me on top of him before kissing my lips. "You've had my heart for a long time, baby girl. I was just waiting for you to accept it. Are you ready?"

"I am."

"About fuckin' time." He popped me on my ass. "Now, let me go make sure this woman ain't fuck up my shit."

"Are you sure you're ready to end things with her? I'm not about to be on no back-and-forth shit."

"Unfortunately for Vida, she was just a placeholder."

After another kiss, he slid from underneath me and got out of bed, then headed to the bathroom. About ten minutes later, he was dressed in some of his clothes that he had in my extra bedroom. Every time he came to visit, he left something.

"Jae, I gotta go."

"Bye."

"You still got a damn attitude? What the hell are you worried about?"

"I don't see why you gotta go back to the hotel right now. Send her ass a text and let her know what's up."

He chuckled. "Damn, Jae. You cold as hell. If nothing else, I need to go get my shit. Are you really worried?"

I didn't want to admit that I was a little worried. I'd never talked to Kamden about Vida, and I was unsure about the seriousness of their relationship. I mean, he did bring her to Belize, and she was here in Seattle. That seemed kind of serious. As I thought about how I wanted to answer his question, he yanked the comforter away from my body and pulled me to the edge of the bed.

"Kam, what the fuck?"

Before I could figure out what the hell he was doing, his head was buried between my legs, and his mouth latched on to my pussy.

"Oh shit!" I screamed.

After being celibate for close to two years, my pussy was sensitive as hell. He could probably blow on it and I'd wet this whole bed up. The way he feasted on my button had me running.

"Naw, come back here," Kamden said, clamping his arms around my thighs.

He licked, sucked, dipped, dived, and flicked his tongue on every nerve ending that existed in and around my pussy. When my climax began to build, I was almost afraid that he would drown because I knew it would be a river. Before I could warn him, the dam broke.

"Ahhhh, Kam, shit!"

The nigga just wouldn't let up. My hands went to his head, and I squirmed as I tried to push him away. Finally, he had mercy on me and came up for air. While I caught my breath, I could feel him hovering over me.

"What the fuck you think is about to happen when I go to this hotel? I'm fresh up outta your pussy, and now, your pussy juice is all over my face and on my breath. Check your fuckin' attitude and act like you heard me tell you I love your ass." He slapped my ass, hard, then said, "Now, come lock up and turn on the alarm."

I could barely move but managed to put on the T-shirt I was

wearing last night. When I got to the front door, he was leaning against it.

"You straight? I mean, will you be good by yourself?"

"I already told you. I'm licensed to carry. If he comes back, I'll shoot his ass."

He pulled his head back and gave me a shocked expression, then nodded his head. "Hopefully, it doesn't come to that. But if it does, light his ass up, baby girl."

After kissing my forehead, my nose, then my lips, he was gone... with the scent of my pussy spilling from his pores.

KAMDEN

as soon as I got in the Uber, I called Vida. It went straight to voicemail. I couldn't tell if she had me blocked or ignored my call. I tried a few more times and got the same result. I scrolled through the messages that she'd sent during the wee hours of the morning.

V: Where are you?

V: Are you okay?

V: Did something happen?

It was clear that initially she was worried, and I felt kinda bad about that. However, she was pissed now.

V: You ain't shit!

V: I knew your ass was lying.

V: Why bring me here just to leave me in the hotel to go fuck your 'best friend'.

V: Fuck you! Don't even bother contacting me. I'm leaving. I'm done with your trifling ass. Fuck ass nigga!

When I left Vida at the hotel, I had no intention of staying with Jaelynn the whole night. Vida had every right to be pissed off, and I had no defense. That last text she'd sent about ten minutes ago.

Maybe I'd make it to the hotel before she left. I at least wanted to apologize and make sure she was straight. I exited out of her text thread and went to another.

Me: *Wassup, bruh. I need a favor.*
Myles: *Wassup?*
Me: *I'm in town. Can we meet up?*
Myles: *Give me a couple hours.*
Me: *Cool.*

He replied with his address, and I exited out of the thread. A few minutes later, I was at the hotel. I moved quickly, hoping to catch Vida before she left. When I got to our room, I heard her talking to someone on speaker.

"No, I'm not waiting," she said.

"Vida, he could have a legitimate reason. From what you told me about him, Kamden doesn't seem like the kind of dude that be on bullshit," the woman's voice said.

"Cara, I didn't think so either. I could have stayed with my ex for this shit."

"Why would he bring you to Seattle to leave you alone in the hotel? It doesn't make sense." Cara reasoned.

"I don't know, and I don't give a damn. I found a flight that's leaving in a few hours. I gotta make sure I got all my shit so I can go. Can you pick me up from the airport?"

"I gotchu. Text me the details."

I slid my key card in the door and pushed it open. If looks could kill, Vida's ass would be a murderer.

"Wow!" was all she said, shaking her head.

I stepped into the room and let the door close behind me.

"Vida, I fucked up. I'm not gon' even try to make excuses."

"Good, because I wouldn't believe none of that shit anyway. I'm leaving so you can go be with your *best friend.*"

"At least let me reimburse you for your ticket," I offered as I stepped further into the room.

"Damn," she said, softly. "You not even gon' try to stop me from leaving."

"I mean..." I shrugged my shoulders.

"You are one fucked-up individual... not even gon' try to cover the shit up... couldn't even take a fuckin' shower when you crawled up outta her pussy! I can smell her all over you. I hope that shit was worth it."

Oh, it definitely was.

She shook her head in disgust and continued throwing stuff in her bag.

"What's your Cash App, and how much was your ticket?"

"I don't want shit from you. I wanted to believe that you were different, and I gave you the benefit of the doubt. I knew all that best friend shit was a lie. I saw the way y'all looked at each other, but I let that shit ride. That was my mistake, though. It was fun while it lasted."

"At least send me a text and let me know you made it back safely."

"Fuck you, Kamden. Have a nice life!"

She tossed the room key card on the bed and pushed past me, hitting me with her bag. I couldn't find it in me to argue with her or go after her. It would be pointless.

A little over an hour later, I had showered and gathered my belongings. I was on my way down to check out a day earlier since I'd be spending my last night in town with Jaelynn. As I waited for the next available person at the front desk, a text from Myles came through, letting me know that he was home. I ordered an Uber, then turned in the key cards.

Myles lived about twenty minutes from downtown Seattle, where the hotel was. When I arrived, I grabbed my duffle bag and got out. He was already waiting at the door.

"Damn, nigga! I ain't know you was comin' to stay," he expressed, looking at my bag.

"Naw, I ain't staying here. It's a long story, though."

I followed him inside, leaving my bag by the door. He led me to the kitchen, and I sat at the breakfast bar.

"You want a drink or something, bruh?"

"Naw, I'm straight."

"Cool. Wassup?"

"You know anything about Drake, Jaelynn's ex?"

He looked intrigued. "Lil' bit. Why? Wassup?"

"I need to find him."

"I can arrange that. I'm gon' need a lil' more info before I do, though."

"She told me some shit in confidence, and I don't wanna break that. Just know that if you knew, you'd probably kill his ass."

The expression on his face turned to anger. "If you saying what it sounds like you saying, I've killed niggas for much less. I ain't got no problem makin' his ass disappear. You ain't even gotta get your hands dirty."

"Naw, I'm cool with my hands getting dirty."

"You sure about that?"

"Positive."

"Okay." He nodded in understanding. "I gotchu."

Myles made one phone call, and an hour later, we were in a dimly lit warehouse. I knew Myles was into some shit that he was trying to step away from, but it was clear that he hadn't quite separated himself yet. We walked to the back, where a group of niggas stood in a circle. Drake was sitting in a chair in the center, with his arms tied behind his back. When he saw me, he frowned.

"Who the fuck are you?" he asked, trying to sound hard.

"Don't worry about who the fuck I am. Just know I got a problem with niggas that can't take no for an answer."

"What the fuck you talking about?"

"Untie him," I demanded to anyone who would do it.

One of the guys untied him and he stood.

"This ass whooping is for Jaelynn."

That was his only warning he got before I punched his ass in the face. He was slightly caught off guard but recovered quickly. From then, it was on. Just as I thought, Drake was a weak ass nigga, and he barely landed a punch while I landed all of mine. I threw head and body blows, and it didn't take long for him to fall to his knees, spitting up blood. I could have left him tied up, but I wanted this to be a fair fight. I kicked him repeatedly, some landed in his stomach, a few in his face.

I heard Myles say, "That's enough."

But I was in a zone, and I wanted to be the person that caused him to take his last breath. My foot kept making contact until I felt someone put me in a bear hug from behind and pull me away.

"What the fuck?" I shouted.

"I said that's enough. Y'all know what to do," Myles tossed behind him before dragging me out the building.

Once we were in his car, we rode in silence for a few minutes before I said, "Why didn't you let me end him?"

He took his eyes off the road for a moment and glanced at me before responding, "I got people that do that kinda shit on the regular and sleep peacefully at night. That ain't you, bruh. I didn't want his blood on your hands."

"I told you I was good with it."

"But I wasn't. Where to?"

"Jaelynn."

He nodded his head.

"When you go inside, I need you to take off all your clothes, shoes included, put them in a bag, and bring them to the door. I'll come get them."

This time, I nodded. No more words were spoken until he pulled in front of Jaelynn's house.

When I got out, I leaned inside the car and said, "Give me two minutes." I grabbed my duffle bag out the back seat before heading inside.

I hadn't communicated with Jaelynn since I left this morning, but when I approached the door, she was standing there waiting for me. She barely let me get inside before the questions started.

"Where have you been? Why were you with Myles?"

I kissed her cheek without touching her with my hands.

"I had some shit I needed to take care of."

"With Myles? Oh my God! What happened to your face?"

She reached up and touched my jaw, near my lip. I moved my head and touched the same spot. Drake did actually connect a couple of times. I hadn't realized it, because the shit didn't hurt. She caught sight of my hands, and her eyes got wide.

"Kam, what the fuck happened?"

I moved around her in an effort to avoid this conversation.

"I'm about to take a shower."

She followed me to her bedroom and got in front of me.

"Kam, what are you hiding? What did you do?"

I put my bag on the floor at the foot of her bed and began to get undressed. Jaelynn kept her eyes on me while I avoided hers. When I got down to my underwear, I finally looked at her.

"I'm gon' say this, and then I don't want to talk about this shit again. Do you understand?"

She nodded.

"I'm not playing, Jae. Don't ask me shit else about this again. Not now, not ever!"

She looked at me with wide eyes, contemplating whether or not she wanted to agree. While she decided, I took off my last piece of clothing, found a pair of sweats in my bag, and slipped them on. Gathering up all my clothes, shoes included, I went to the kitchen, found a plastic bag and put everything inside. When I opened the door, Myles was approaching.

"Thanks, bruh," I said, handing him the bag.

"No thanks needed. That's baby sis. She won't have to worry about that nigga again."

Not asking what he meant, I nodded in understanding. I

connected my fist with his and closed the door. When I turned around, Jaelynn was right behind me.

"Okay, I won't ask you about it again."

I looked her directly in her eyes and said, "That nigga is no longer a problem. You won't be running into him while you're out, he can't call you, and there will be no more pop-ups in the middle of the night."

Kissing her forehead, her nose, and her lips, I left her to her thoughts and went to take a shower.

JAELYNN

*W*hen Kamden left, I went back to sleep for a couple of hours, and it was some of the best sleep I'd gotten in a long time. But I woke up slightly overwhelmed when I realized the meaning of all that had transpired in the last twelve hours.

For two years, I'd been dealing with the emotional scars of being raped, too afraid and embarrassed to tell a soul. I planned to take that secret to the grave, but telling Kamden did give me some level of comfort. Maybe going to therapy would do me some good.

I kept myself busy for most of the day. After doing some light cleaning, including putting a fresh set of sheets on my bed, I showered and called Braelynn and Myla. I figured I'd better tell them about me and Kamden before they found out from their husbands.

"Hey, Jae! Happy New Year!" Braelynn answered.

"Hey, Brae! Happy New Year to you, too. Hold on so I can call My."

I put her on hold and called Myla, then merged the two calls.

"Happy New Year, Jae!" Myla answered. "You gon' have to excuse this noise. Your niece and nephew are on a warpath."

"Do I need to come and get my babies?" Braelynn offered.

"Hey, Brae! Yup! Come get their busy asses."

"You know I would, but we're still unpacking. Our house is a mess."

Braelynn and Kyree had just bought a house, not far from Myla and Kolby. Instead of bringing the new year in partying, they spent it moving and unpacking.

"I'll take a rain check. As soon as y'all get settled, I'm dropping their asses off for a week." Myla joked.

"My, please. You couldn't be away from them that long." I added.

"And Kolby would have a fit, anyway. So what's up, sis. Did you have fun last night?" Braelynn asked, changing the subject.

"Umm, I can't say that I did."

"What the hell happened?" they both asked, alarmed.

"Before I tell y'all that, there's something else I need to say."

"We're listening," Braelynn said.

"I'm in love with Kamden," I confessed.

After a moment of silence, both of those heffas busted out laughing.

"What the hell is so funny?"

"You," Myla said.

"Yeah! Tell us something we don't know." Braelynn added.

"Whatever! Y'all didn't know."

"Girl, anyone with eyes could see that y'all are in love with each other. Well, maybe except poor Vida," Myla said.

"Ha! That girl knows. She's just in denial."

"Well, I finally told him," I confessed.

"For real?"

"You did?"

"I did. Last night was crazy. Drake was there, and he couldn't help but be the asshole that he is. We got into it, and he fucked up my whole vibe. I left the club, angry and pissed off at Drake. A couple of hours later, Kamden was knocking on the door."

"Wait... didn't you say he was bringing Vida to Seattle?" came from Braelynn.

"He did. He took her back to the hotel and told her that he needed to check on me. She gave him an ultimatum, and he left her ass there."

"Damnnnn," they sang.

"Anyway, one thing led to another, and now we're together," I told them.

"Oh, hell naw. We need more details than that. Run that shit from the beginning," Braelynn demanded.

"Don't leave out a single thing," Myla added.

I told them everything that went down last night and early this morning, leaving out everything about the rape, of course. They were ecstatic about Kamden and I finally succumbing to our feelings for each other.

After hanging up with them, I decided to swing by my mom's house to get a plate for me and Kamden. She made black-eyed peas, cornbread, ham, and macaroni and cheese. When I arrived, Uncle David was there, along with his girlfriend, Vivian.

"Happy New Year, everyone!" I shouted when I walked into the dining room.

Everyone returned the sentiment, and we conversed a bit before I went to the kitchen to fix our plates. My mom came in after me and leaned against the counter. When I felt her gaze on me, I looked at her.

"Why are you staring at me?"

"You seem different."

"Different? How?"

"I don't know. Your spirit seems... lighter. What happened last night?"

How do moms know every damn thing?

I wrapped both plates in aluminum foil and set them on the counter before turning and leaning against it.

"What makes you think something happened last night?"

"Because I know my daughter. Now, spill it."

After a deep breath, I said, "Kamden and I are... a thing," almost giddy at my confession. I could feel my smile spreading from ear to ear.

"Yes!" she cheered and pulled me into a hug. "About damn time. You two have been tiptoeing around your feelings for each other for too damn long. I guess I should get ready for another wedding because those Ross boys don't play."

"Oh my God, Mom. It hasn't been a full twenty-four hours. Slow down on the wedding talk."

"I said what I said. Kamden might be the baby boy, but I have a feeling he knows more about what he wants than his brothers. You just wait and see."

She was so happy. You would have thought I'd told her that Kamden and I were already engaged. She hugged me again and, of course, went to the family room to announce the news to Uncle David and Vivian.

"Oh, hell," Uncle David said. "Let me get my tux ready."

My mom looked at me, and I chuckled while shaking my head. After spending a little time with them, I stopped by the pharmacy to pick up a Plan B pill and some condoms since I wasn't on birth control and Kamden was out here shooting up the club. Although he'd mentioned that he wanted multiple kids, we were speaking generally. Everything happened so fast last night that I wasn't so sure he realized that he didn't wrap up. And he definitely didn't ask me about birth control.

I hadn't heard from him all day, and it took everything in me not to text him. I wanted to give him the time he needed to handle his situation with Vida.

Not long after I got home, I heard a car out front. I was a bit surprised to see Myles dropping Kamden off. I opened the front door and looked on as they said their goodbyes. As soon as he stepped foot inside, I grilled him with questions.

"Where have you been? Why were you with Myles?"

He kissed my cheek.

"I had some shit I needed to take care of," was all he said.

What would he have to take care of with Myles?

"With Myles? Oh my God! What happened to your face?"

His jaw, near his lips, was swollen, and there looked to be dry blood in the area. I touched it, and when he grabbed my wrist, I noticed there was blood on his hand as well.

"Kam, what the fuck happened?"

He moved past me and headed toward my bedroom, and I followed him.

"I'm about to take a shower," he said, not answering any of my questions.

"Kam, what are you hiding? What did you do?"

He dropped his duffle bag and started to undress. I was getting annoyed because he wasn't saying shit. Finally, he stopped what he was doing and looked me in my eyes.

"I'm gon' say this, and then I don't want to talk about this shit again. Do you understand?"

His eyes were dark, and it scared me a little. I wasn't sure if I still wanted to know.

"I'm not playing, Jae. Don't ask me shit else about this again. Not now, not ever," he spoke firmly.

When I didn't reply, he continued getting undressed, then got a pair of sweats from his bag and put them on. After he gathered up his clothes and shoes, I followed him to the kitchen and watched him put everything in a plastic bag.

I was right behind him when he went to the door and handed Myles the bag of clothes. *Damn! He's getting rid of evidence.* They exchanged some words, and Kamden closed and locked the door. When he turned around, I was right behind his ass.

"Okay, I won't ask you about it again."

"That nigga is no longer a problem. You won't be running into him while you're out, he can't call you, and there will be no more pop-ups in the middle of the night." He kissed my forehead, nose, then lips, and walked away like he hadn't said shit.

What did he do? I got questions!

I stripped down so I could join him in the shower. He was facing the other direction and turned around when I opened the shower door.

As soon as I stepped in, he pinned me against the wall and covered my mouth with his, forcing his tongue inside. His hand squeezed my neck firmly, but not too hard. He kissed me in such a way that took my breath away. It was hard and aggressive yet, somehow, still gentle. The only reason I didn't suffocate was because I drew my breath from his.

I wrapped my arms around his neck and legs around his waist. When he pressed his hardness against my clit and ground against it, I knew that my climax would come without penetration. Finally, he tore his mouth away from mine and pressed his forehead against mine.

"I've been waiting a long time to love you," he mumbled against my lips. "I'll do anything to keep you safe."

Is he trying to tell me something?

"Do hear me?"

I nodded and moaned as he continued to grind.

"I'll do anything."

With those words, I hit my peak and damn near gave myself a concussion when I flung my head back against the wall. Kamden didn't waste a second entering my soaked walls.

"Fuck," he groaned into my neck.

His tongue tickled my neck before he latched on, I'm sure, marking me up. He bent his knees and stroked me deeply, causing me to press my hand against his chest.

"Ahh, Kam, it's too deep."

"Naw, baby girl. Take all this dick."

Instead of taking it easy, he went deeper. My body was

confused by the pain and pleasure it was experiencing. *How could something hurt and feel this good simultaneously?*

Our mouths connected again, and the overwhelming sensations I felt from our kiss sent me over the top. The tingling began at my toes and shot straight to my G-spot.

"Kam, babe, I'm cummin'!"

"Not yet, Jae. Hold that shit."

Wait! What?

"I—shh—oh my gaa—"

"Hold it, Jae!"

But why though?

Somehow, my pleasure went to another level. Kamden's tongue swirled inside my ear, and he pinched one of my nipples while delivering slow, deep strokes. Fuck whatever this nigga was talking about. I was about to explode. I simply could not hold it.

"Kam, please! I can't—"

"You ready to cum with me, Jae?"

"Yes!"

"Let that shit go, baby girl."

The combination of his dick throbbing and my pussy pulsing at the same damn time... *whew!* It was a feeling like no other. Once we were depleted, our chests heaved up and down, and his head fell against my shoulder. We exchanged no words as we came down from our high. He gently removed himself from my domain and let my legs slide down until my feet hit the floor. Surprisingly, the water was still warm, and we quickly bathed ourselves.

When we got out, I dried off and lathered up in my body butter and dressed in a T-shirt and boy shorts while Kam threw on a pair of sweats.

"I got us a plate from my mom's house. You hungry?"

"Hell, yeah. I ain't ate shit but you today, and that wore off a long time ago."

"Whatever, nasty ass. How'd everything go with Vida?"

He sat at the kitchen table while I warmed his food in the microwave.

"Shit! Probably exactly how you think. She was pissed. Told me I was a fucked-up individual and that she could smell your pussy on me."

My mouth formed the letter "O", but nothing came out.

"Yep! I offered to pay for her flight, but she said she didn't want shit from me. I'm guessing she got back to Chicago okay. I haven't heard from her."

"Were you expecting to?"

"Not really, but I did tell her to let me know she got back safely."

I gave him his plate and a bottle of water, then warmed mine. By the time I sat down with my food, Kamden was halfway done.

"I guess you were hungry. You didn't even bless the food."

"I told you I was starving. My bad, Lord. A nigga was hungry."

I shook my head at his crazy ass before taking my first bite. We ate in silence for a few minutes before I said, "I talked to Brae and My about us."

"Oh yeah? What'd you tell them?"

"Almost everything."

He looked up from his plate, understanding exactly what I left out.

"What'd they say?"

"They weren't surprised. Claimed they knew all along that I was in love with you."

He looked up from his plate. "How long have you been in love with me, baby girl?"

I shrugged my shoulders because I truly didn't know. I was in denial for a long time. "The jury is still out on that, but I was finally ready to tell you at the wedding."

He closed his eyes and put his head down. When he looked up at me again, I saw sadness in his eyes.

"I knew I should have gone after you that night. Kyree and Kolby stopped me."

"It was probably for the best. I'm not sure how Vida would have handled all that while in another country."

"I had a miserable ass time for the rest of our stay. You were avoiding me, which made me irritable. Vida was constantly trying to figure what was wrong because, as much as I tried to have a good time, my mood was fucked."

"You shouldn't have brought her ass anyway," I said with a pout.

"That wasn't part of the plan, but when I said something to her about it, she invited herself and paid for her own tickets. Shit, you wasn't giving me no play, so I figured why not."

"Anyway, I don't wanna talk about her anymore."

"You're the one that brought her up." He teased.

"Well, now I'm changing the subject. I told my mom and Uncle David about us, too."

"Damn, Jae. You couldn't wait to spread the news, huh?"

"Is that a problem?" I pretended to be hurt.

"Hell naw! We gon' make our first Instagram post tonight. I gotta shut down all them niggas in your DMs."

"Boy, please. My DMs is like the Sahara Desert. Ain't shit happening in there."

"Yeah, I bet. What'd the family say?"

"My mom picked up on something as soon as I got there. She said my spirit was lighter and started questioning me. When I finally told her, she said she'd better start getting ready for another wedding."

He smiled but didn't say anything.

"I told her to slow all that down. We gotta figure out if we can be together first."

"Ain't shit to figure out, Jae. I've been waiting too fuckin' long to make you mine, but I don't believe in forcing things. I believe things happen when they're supposed to. I ain't gon' lie, baby girl... I was starting to lose hope that there would ever be an us."

My eyes got wide. "Really?"

"C'mere."

I got up, and he moved his chair back so I could sit on his lap.

"When you friend-zoned me, I thought to myself, *we can't be friends*. But I was willing to do whatever to keep you in my life. As time progressed and you didn't seem to be any closer to changing your mind about that, I settled into our friendship, and I enjoyed it. I still wanted more, but you didn't. So yeah, I lost a little hope. Only about this much, though." He held his thumb and index finger up with only a sliver of space between them.

"I always wanted more, but I wasn't ready."

"Everything happens when it's supposed to," he repeated.

I wrapped my arms around his neck and leaned into his lips. We enjoyed a savory kiss for a little while, until I started to get hot and bothered. When I pulled away, his mouth followed mine, and he continued to peck my lips, luring me into another few minutes of tantalizing tongue wrestling.

Kamden had an early flight, so the rest of the evening, we watched a little Netflix and did a lot of *chilling*. As much as I wished he could stay, my vagina could definitely use a break.

KAMDEN

The early flight was a good idea when Vida was with me. Now... not so much. It almost pained me when I removed myself from in between Jaelynn's legs. I could literally live there. I opted to shower alone because I'd miss my flight if she joined me. She'd fallen back to sleep by the time I got out. I planted kisses along her jawline and neck to wake her up.

"Kammm, I'm tiirrred," she whined.

"I know, baby girl, but you gotta get up. Are you showering?"

"Not if I can sleep longer if I don't. It's too early."

I couldn't help but laugh at her, knowing good and well that it was my fault that she was so tired. Knowing that I wouldn't see her for a few weeks had us up damn near all night. Even with that, I still had to have another dose when my alarm went off.

After getting dressed and eating a bowl of cereal, I went back to wake Jaelynn up. She begrudgingly got up, took care of her basic hygiene, then slid on some leggings and a hoodie. Her hair was back in its natural state of curls, and she put it in a puff on the top of her head.

"I'm ready," she said.

I could hear the sadness in her voice. I pulled her into my arms, and she buried her head in my chest.

"Babe, don't be sad. I wish I could stay longer, but I didn't arrange it ahead of time with my crew. You know you don't have to wait until the twins' birthday to come out."

"I'll be there a week before their birthday, and I'm staying for a month to get ready for the fashion show. I already booked my flight, and I don't want to pay to have to change it."

"If you want to come sooner, let me know. I'll pay for it. Give me a kiss."

She lifted her head and got on her tiptoes while I leaned down until our lips connected.

"You good?" I asked.

"No, but I'll be fine. Can you grab my purse behind you?"

I turned around and reached for her purse, but apparently, I didn't have a good grip on it. It fell to the floor, with some of the contents spilling out.

"Shit! My bad."

We both kneeled down to pick everything up. I thought my eyes were deceiving me when I saw a box that read Plan B. Picking it up, I looked back and forth between Jaelynn and the box.

"What the fuck is this?" I said in an even tone, trying to control the anger I felt building.

She reached for it, and I moved my hand away.

"Is this what the fuck you on? A Plan B?"

"I'm not on birth control, and we haven't used any protection. I bought these, too, but I forgot about them." She held up a box of condoms.

Fuck those condoms. "You trying to kill my baby?"

"What? No, I just—we didn't use—I was gonna take it as a precaution."

"The fuck, Jae? A precaution for what?"

"Kam, we've been fucking like rabbits. We haven't talked about—"

"Don't tell that fuckin' lie, Jae. You know I want kids."

"We've been together for five minutes, Kam. Everything happened so fast. I—"

"So fast? I've *been* in love with your ass. I would marry you right fuckin' now! Today! That's what the fuck I'm on. Clearly, we not on the same page."

I threw that Plan B box against the wall across the room. I had to get away from her before I said or did some shit I couldn't take back.

"I don't need a ride," I told her as I took out my phone to request an Uber.

"Kam, wait."

I had my hand on the door handle, and she touched my shoulder. "You can't leave like this. I'm sorry. I wasn't thinking."

"Yeah, you were. That's what's so fucked up about it."

I left without a glance back and walked to the curb to wait for the Uber. When the car pulled up, I got in the back seat. It was then that I looked back at the house, and I saw Jaelynn standing at the door. I shook my head in disappointment as we drove away.

WHEN I GOT HOME, both my brothers were in my apartment waiting for me. Telling them to use their key for emergencies only meant absolutely nothing.

"What the hell y'all niggas doing here?"

"What's with the hostility? We came to congratulate you on finally getting your girl," Kyree said.

"I would think you'd be in a better mood." Kolby added.

"I appreciate the congratulatory wishes. Can y'all leave now?"

"Damn, bruh! Who pissed in your cheerios?" Kolby asked.

"Nobody. It's been a long couple of days, and I'm tired. I'm going to bed. Lock up when you leave."

I headed down the hall in the direction of my bedroom. Kyree hopped in front of me before I made it.

"Hold up, bruh." He put his hand on my shoulder and turned me around, guiding me to the living room.

We sat on the couch, while Kolby sat in the sofa chair. They both looked at me expectantly, but I didn't have shit to say.

"Tell us wassup?" Kyree said.

When I didn't say anything, Kolby said, "Are you and Jae together? As in an official couple?"

"I'd like to say that we are, but when I left her house, I wasn't so sure."

"Start from the beginning. You confusing the hell outta us," Kyree admitted.

"Some shit went down at the club on New Year's Eve, with her ex—"

"Is that where that bruise on your face came from?" Kyree interrupted.

Shit!

"No. That's another story for another time. Anyway, Jaelynn ended up leaving, and I was worried. I took Vida back to the hotel and left her there to check on Jae. Obviously, Vida was pissed, but y'all know how I feel about Jae, so going to see about her was a no-brainer. I ended up staying all night, and... things happened. Between that night and this morning, things happened multiple times."

"Hold up!" Kolby held his hand up. "Vida let you leave her at the hotel *all night?*"

I nodded and shrugged my shoulders. "When I went back, she was pissed and packing her shit. She caught a flight back yesterday morning."

"So what the hell happened between you and Jae?" Kyree asked.

I shook my head and exhaled. Thinking about the shit pissed me off.

"She's not on birth control, and I didn't wrap up. This morning, the Plan B pill box fell out of her purse."

"Ohhhhh," they both said.

"Yeah, I was pissed off."

"I'm guessing if she's pregnant, you cool with that?" Kyree questioned.

"Hell yeah! I know Jae is my wife, and y'all know I want a handful of kids by the time I'm thirty-five. My clock is ticking."

"First of all, bruh, you sound like a damn woman, talking about your clock is ticking. Secondly, does she know that? I mean, have y'all discussed this?" Kolby inquired.

"Jae and I have talked about damn near everything. She knows."

"Yeah, but y'all was on some friends shit, and your ass wanting a starting lineup didn't mean shit to her when y'all was just friends. Maybe she's not ready." Kyree reasoned.

"Was she planning to take the pill or had she already taken it?" Kolby asked.

"I don't remember if the box was open or not. I don't think she'd taken it yet. I was so pissed. I threw the box across the room and left. I ended up taking an Uber to the airport."

"Damn, all this happened this morning?" came from Kolby.

"As we were getting ready to leave for the airport."

"I mean, I get why you're upset," Kyree began, "but you have to put yourself in her shoes. Things between y'all are still new—"

I began shaking my head because I wasn't trying to hear that shit.

"Why are you shaking your head? Your relationship is barely forty-eight hours old." He continued.

"Naw, that's not true. Us becoming intimate is new, but our relationship is just as solid as yours with your wives. I know her better than anybody else, and she knows me just as well. There's nothing she can say to make me believe that she thought I'd want her to take a damn Plan B... not a damn thing."

I stood from the couch, letting them know that I was done talking about the shit.

"Y'all can let yourselves out."

"You can tell us about that bruise on your face and the cuts on your hands another time," one of them said.

I couldn't tell who because I was going into my room. That was a conversation I would be avoiding at all costs.

A couple of hours later, I'd showered, unpacked, started a load of laundry, and was sitting comfortably on my couch with my laptop. While I was in the process of making the work schedule for my crew, I received a text message from Jaelynn.

Jae: Are you home?

Me: Yep.

Jae: Can we talk?

Me: I'm kinda busy right now.

I saw the dots appear, then disappear a few times, but a text never came through. I was still in my feelings about the situation and wasn't sure when I would feel up to talking to her. I simply needed some time.

JAELYNN

a few days had passed, and I still hadn't talked to Kamden. I reached out to him a few more times, but he didn't answer my calls and only replied to my texts with one or two words. I wasn't sure how to take his lack of communication. Obviously, he needed some space. *But how much space, and for how long?*

Apparently, he'd spoken to his brothers about what happened, and of course, they talked to their wives. A few nights ago, Braelynn and Myla FaceTimed me and gave their thoughts on what they'd been told.

"Jae, if you don't want kids, why didn't you make him wrap it up?" Braelynn asked.

"Obviously, I wasn't thinking, Brae. And it's not that I don't want kids."

"What is it then?" asked Myla.

"The first time we had sex, I thought I was dreaming."

"Damn, it was that good?" came from Myla.

"Yeah, it was, but I've probably had a hundred dreams about fucking Kamden. I thought this was just another one. When I woke up, I was straddling him, and he was still hard inside of me."

"*Dammmnnn!*" *they said simultaneously.*

"*Exactly! When I realized what had happened, I tried to get up. But he wasn't having that shit. Next thing I know, we were at it again. So, the way the shit went down, I didn't have time to think about it.*"

"*I guess not,*" *Myla commented.*

"*When did you get the Plan B?*" *Braelynn questioned.*

"*Later that day. I bought some condoms, too. My intention was for us to use them if we had sex again, but after Myles dropped him off—*"

"*Why was he with Myles?*" *Myla asked.*

Shit!

"*Umm, I didn't really ask. I think he just gave him a ride. But anyway, the next time we did it was in the shower, and at that point, I'd forgotten about the condoms and the Plan B.*"

"*Well, from what Kyree said, Kamden is real fucked up about it.*"

"*Yeah, that's what Kolby said, too.*"

"*I've been trying to talk to him, but he won't pick up any of my calls. I don't want to text him about it because it's not the kind of conversation you have over text. He's just being stubborn, and the shit is getting annoying.*"

"*Can you blame him?*" *Myla said, sounding very judgmental.*

"*You know what? I'll talk to y'all later.*"

I ended the call and put my phone on do not disturb.

I respected them both, but from the beginning of the conversation, I could tell that they thought I was wrong for even considering taking the damn pill. I hadn't talked to them since, although they had called and texted me a few times, apologizing.

To keep my mind off Kamden, I'd been focusing my mental and emotional health, and MyLynn's Bedroom Boutique. Taking Kamden's advice, I found a therapist, Dr. Femi, who happened to be a Black woman. I'd only had one visit so far, but it had definitely helped. The main thing I took from talking with her was that the rape wasn't my fault. The logical side of my brain had always known that; however, I still found myself taking the blame sometimes.

She explained that most victims, of any crime, tend to blame themselves. Constantly, they'd ask themselves where they went wrong or what they could have done differently. Once the victim realized that the only person to blame was the person that committed the crime, a huge weight was lifted from their shoulders, and the healing process could begin.

MyLynn's Bedroom Boutique had been keeping me busy. There were several ladies that had posted pictures of themselves in some of our pieces and tagged our Instagram page. I reached out to them to see if they were interested in being brand ambassadors. Communicating back and forth with them took longer than I anticipated, but I was thankful for the distraction.

We were also having a Valentine's Day fashion show in Chicago, and I spent some time looking through pictures of models that were submitted. When my cell phone chimed, my heart skipped a beat. Unfortunately, it wasn't Kamden.

Danae: Did you hear about Drake?

Me: No

Danae: They found his body... well, what was left of it.

Me: What?

Instead of replying, she called me.

"Where'd you hear that?" I asked as soon as I picked up.

"On the news. Apparently, he'd been missing since New Year's Day. They found him in his car, both burned to a crisp."

"Oh my God!"

"I know, right? That shit is crazy. I mean, Drake was an asshole, but damn!"

I was literally speechless. *Drake is... dead?* Suddenly, I thought about the things Kamden said, and did, the day that Myles dropped him off.

"That nigga is no longer a problem. You won't be running into

him while you're out, he can't call you, and there will be no more pop-ups in the middle of the night." I recalled he also gave his clothes to Myles to get rid of.

"Nae, I gotta go." I ended the call and immediately called Kamden. "Please, Kam, pick up."

"Wassup, Jae," he answered, dryly.

"What did you do with Myles the other day?"

"What?"

"Myles, Kam. Why were you with Myles?"

"What did I tell you?"

"I know, but—"

"No!" he shouted. "I told you not to ask me about that shit."

"Fine!"

I hung up the phone and called Myles.

"Wassup, Jae," he answered.

"What did you and Kam do?"

"What are you talkin' about?"

"You know what I'm talking about, Myles."

"If Kam didn't tell you, then he must not want you to know. It ain't my place, sweetheart."

"Seriously? You're like my brother. You barely know Kam."

"Still not my place. But you good otherwise? You know I'm here if you ever need anything."

I released a frustrated breath. "I'm fine. I gotta go."

I ended the call and sat silently for a few minutes, trying to get my thoughts together. Based on what Kamden said to me after Myles dropped him off, the disposing of his clothes, and the cuts and bruises that he had, I had a feeling Kamden and Myles had something to do with what happened to Drake. *Were they responsible for his death?* I had so many questions that I knew I'd probably never get answered.

My mental was shot, and I couldn't focus on the work that I was doing. It wasn't that I cared about Drake. He deserved to die for what he did to me. I was concerned about Kamden and Myles. *What if Drake's death somehow leads back to them?*

KAMDEN

*A*lmost two weeks had flown by, and I was still in my fuckin' feelings. Every time I thought about the possibility of Jaelynn being pregnant and her taking a damn Plan B, I got pissed off all over again. It was like everything I thought I knew about her was wrong.

She'd completely given up on calling me but had been reaching out to me a few times a day through text. I replied with as few words possible. However, the last couple of days, I hadn't heard anything from her. Even though I was still pissed off, hearing from her did give me some comfort. I was debating on whether or not I needed to bite the bullet and reach out to her.

The months of November through February were very busy for cleaning companies. I had hired some people through a temporary agency to help keep up with the demand. Since I'd started Ross Cleaning and Janitorial Services, I rarely worked with my crews. However, these winter months were brutal, and I worked with them damn near every day.

I'd been working so much that one would think I wouldn't have time to think about Jaelynn. Me being busy *and* pissed off at her didn't stop her from invading my mind. Love was crazy like that, I guess.

My day ended a bit later than usual. By the time I was home and showered, it was about eight o'clock. I put a frozen pizza in the oven and chilled on the couch, watching ESPN, while I waited for my pizza. Jaelynn was still heavy on my mind, so I decided to go ahead and call her. Just as I picked up my phone, there was a knock on my door.

"I know damn well these niggas ain't actually knocking on the door," I said out loud, thinking it was one or both of my brothers.

When I looked out of the peephole, I was shocked at who I saw. I cautiously opened the door and stood face-to-face with Vida.

"Wassup, V?"

I forgot that I wasn't wearing a shirt or no damn underwear, until Vida's eye's roamed my body. They stopped at the imprint in my sweats, and she licked her lips.

"Vida?"

"Huh? Oh, yeah. Hey."

"You good? You need something?"

"Can I come in? Or are you busy?"

"Yeah, you can come in for a few minutes." I stepped back, leaving enough room for her to enter.

She waited for me to lock the door, then followed me to the kitchen. Before taking a seat at the breakfast bar, she took off her coat and put it on the empty stool next to her.

"I wasn't expecting company, but I got a pizza in the oven if you want some."

"No, I'm good actually."

"Something to drink?"

"No, I'm fine."

I nodded as I washed my hands, then proceeded to take my pizza out of the oven. After I cut it into slices and put some on a plate, I grabbed a bottle of water and went to the breakfast bar. Instead of sitting next to her, I remained standing on the other side.

Vida was wearing a brown V-neck sweater that exposed her ample cleavage. Shit, I had to stop myself from staring and licking my lips.

"So... what brings you by?" I asked, before biting a slice of pizza.

"Us."

"Us?" *There is no us.*

"What happened?"

"Look, V. I'm gon' keep it real. Trying to have a relationship with you, or anyone else, was a mistake."

"Wow!"

"I'm not trying to hurt you. I'm being honest. My feelings for Jaelynn run deep, and they have for a long time. She was on that, 'let's be just friends' shit, and I agreed, even though I wanted to be her man."

"What the fuck were we doing if you wanted to be with someone else the whole time?"

I moved on to my fourth or fifth slice of pizza, not having a lot to say about what she'd just asked

"All I can say is me and you were never gonna work long term, and it had nothing to do with you. I'm in love with Jaelynn," I finally said.

I didn't mean to hurt her feelings, but from the look on her face, that was exactly what I did. I wasn't sure what she expected to gain from her visit. Maybe she was looking for closure.

"Besides, the way you cussed me out at the hotel, I didn't think you cared that much, anyway."

"You lucky all I did was cuss you out. I knew I was done with your ass when you left."

"How? When I left, I was not planning to cheat on you. I truly went to check on my friend. Please know, my intentions were pure."

"Yeah, whatever, nigga!"

I went to the sink to wash the pizza sauce from my hands as she stood and began to slide on her coat. *I guess closure is what she needed.* I headed for the door and waited for her to bundle up, then opened it, using my body to keep it open.

"You may not believe me, but I apologize for how shit went down. You'll be a great woman for a man that ain't in love with somebody else."

When she was standing in front of me, I pulled her into a hug and kissed her forehead.

"Thanks, Kamden. I appreciate your honesty."

When she stepped into the hallway, I turned around and got the shock of my life.

"Jae?" was all I managed to say.

She looked from me to Vida, then back to me, before putting all of her weight on one leg and folding her arms across her chest.

Fuck!

JAELYNN

*J*t had been too damn long since the last time I'd actually spoken to Kamden. I'd lost track of the days, but the number didn't matter. I was beginning to wonder if we could make a relationship work. Only a mere forty-eight hours had passed before we had our first argument, and his stubborn ass didn't even want to discuss the issue. *How were we going to move beyond it if we don't talk about it?*

For the last few days, I chose not to initiate any communication with him, simply to see if he would reach out to me. To my surprise, there was nothing but silence from his end. I didn't sweat it too much, because I knew that I'd be in Chicago today, and I'd be talking to him face-to-face, whether he liked it or not.

My original plan for this trip was to stay with Braelynn for two weeks and Myla for the remainder. When I booked my flight, Kamden was dating Vida, so I knew that staying with him was out of the question. Since I didn't know what the hell was going on between us, staying with him still may not be an option.

Before going to the airport, I went to have breakfast at my favorite twenty-four-hour spot that had the best pancakes on the planet. Hopefully, Ms. Marianne, who was a waitress at the restaurant, was working. When Kyree and Braelynn had a little hiccup in the early stages of their relationship, she gave them some sound advice. Kolby even ended up talking to her when he fucked up with Myla. Ms. Marianne was invited to their wedding, but she couldn't come because her sister was having surgery.

It was early, but there was a nice amount of people there. A hostess seated me, and I looked around for Ms. Marianne. When I didn't see her, I asked the hostess if she was working.

"She is, but this isn't her section. Do you want to move?" she replied.

"Yes, please. If it's not too much trouble."

"No trouble at all. Follow me."

I got up and followed the hostess to another table in Ms. Marianne's section. She was about to give me a menu, but I declined. I already knew what I wanted. She smiled and walked away.

Ms. Marianne approached a few minutes later. I wasn't sure if she would remember me. I'd only seen her once outside of the restaurant, and that was when Kyree proposed to Braelynn.

"Good morning, sweetheart. What can I get for you?"

"Hi, Ms. Marianne. I'd like the pancake special with a large orange juice."

"Okay. I'm gonna go put your order in, and I'll be back with a water... then you can tell me what's bothering you."

She winked at me before she walked away. Between her and Ms. Stella, I didn't know who could read spirits better. I thought my mom was the queen of mood readers, but I think they had her beat. When she returned with the water, she sat in the chair across from me.

"Now what's weighing so heavy on your mind?" she asked.

"Do you remember me?" I asked.

"You're Braelynn's little sister. I remember meeting you when she got engaged."

"Yes, I'm Jaelynn. Wow! I wasn't sure you'd remember me."

"Of course, I do. So what's wrong."

"I know you're working and this is kind of a sensitive topic, so I'll try to tell you the edited version."

She nodded.

"I finally told my best friend that I'm in love with him. Some things happened, and we didn't use... we weren't careful. I wasn't sure if it was intentional on his part, so I was going to take some steps to remedy the situation. He found out before I did anything and got *extremely* upset."

Ms. Marianne looked at me as she took in my words. I wasn't sure if she understood what I was trying to relay, but I hoped so.

"Let me get this straight. You confessed your feelings to your best friend, the two of you had sex, and didn't use protection. Am I right so far?"

"Yes, ma'am."

She looked around the restaurant, then leaned forward before whispering, "Are your pregnant and planning to abort the child?"

"No, no, ma'am. I don't know if I'm pregnant. The day after we had sex, I bought the Plan B pill. It's a pill—"

"I know what it's for. He was upset that you were going to take the pill?"

"Very."

"Were you going to do this without talking to him about it?"

I looked down at the table, embarrassed that I was going to take the pill without speaking to him.

"I was actually but not because I was hiding it from him. I honestly didn't even think it was a big deal. Our relationship is brand new, and—"

"Didn't you say he was your best friend?" Ms. Marianne questioned.

"He is."

"Then what do you mean when you say your relationship is brand new? I imagine you've been friends for some time if he's your best friend."

"Well, yeah, but—"

"No buts, sweetheart. He's not looking at this as a new relationship. That's why he's hurt that you would do something like that behind his back."

"He won't talk to me so I can explain."

"He'll come around, and when you do finally talk to him, be sure to remember to consider how he may have felt when he realized what you planned to do. I'll be right back with your food."

She left before I had a chance to say anything. I knew that when I talked to him, I had to apologize. I just hoped he accepted my apology and we could move on from this. Ms. Marianne returned with my food but didn't sit down.

"I'm gonna give you some time to eat. I'll be back before you leave."

I thoroughly enjoyed my pancakes, bacon, eggs, and seasoned potatoes. About fifteen minutes later, Ms. Marianne returned with a look of surprise on her face.

"I can't believe your little bitty self ate all of that food. You must have been hungry," she commented.

"Hungry and stressed. When I leave here, I'm headed to the airport to catch a flight to Chicago. I'm going to see him later today, and I'm nervous about how it's going to go."

"Listen, Jaelynn. I'm sure you have legitimate reasons for preparing to take those precautions. Be honest with him and communicate those reasons. If you two are meant to be together, he'll understand and forgive you. Okay?"

"Okay. Thank you, Ms. Marianne."

I stood to give her a hug, and she turned to walk away.

"Wait! I need to pay for my food."

"It's on me." She winked and left to help another customer.

BRAELYNN AND MYLA picked me up from the airport, and we went to a restaurant called Slice of Bronzeville for lunch. Once we were seated and had placed our orders, we picked up our conversation from the ride over.

"Are you still mad at us? You're acting kinda funny and shit," Braelynn asked.

Things between me and them had been a little bit strained since our conversation about me taking the morning-after pill. I was more hurt than I was mad, but they'd been working overtime trying to get me to forgive them. I was over it after a couple of days but decided to let them think differently.

"No, I'm over it."

"You know we really didn't mean to sound like we were judging you. Your choice is your choice, and we support you, no matter what," Myla offered.

"It's fine. I know y'all didn't mean anything. How's the party planning going?"

Myla shook her head and rolled her eyes. "Kolby is doing the absolute most. I keep reminding him that they aren't gonna remember a damn thing about the party, but he *insists* on going all out. I don't even wanna talk about it. I just want it to be over."

"It's that bad?" I asked.

"It's that bad," Braelynn answered for Myla. "I told her he's just a proud daddy and to let him do him."

"I'm a proud mama, too, but I know when to chill."

"Well, one more week, and it'll be a distant memory." I reminded her.

The waiter came back with our food, and after saying grace, we dug in. After a few savory bites, I spoke.

"What else is going on? Did y'all look at the pics of the models that I chose?"

"Yeah, but are you trying to avoid talking about Kam?"

"No. I'm not trying to avoid it, but I don't want to talk about him."

"Things any better?" Braelynn asked as if I didn't just say I didn't want to talk about him.

"I'm sure that Kolby and Kyree have given y'all updates."

"Nope! Kam ain't talking to them about it either. Oh, but I have been wanting to ask you something. Kyree said that Kam had bruises on his face and hands when he came back from Seattle. You didn't tell us that he got into a fight. Was it with Drake?"

Shit!

"Not that I know of." I lied. Suddenly, my food became really interesting, as I focused on it instead of them.

"Well, did he say anything? If Kyree saw the bruises, I'm sure you did, too. Did you ask him about them?"

"Umm..." I began but didn't know what to say. I guess they hadn't heard anything about Drake being dead because I sure as hell didn't mention it.

"Umm, what? You know something, don't you?" Myla said with wide, inquiring eyes.

"I—umm—well, see—"

"Spit it out, sis!" Braelynn pushed.

"Drake's dead."

"What? When? How?" came from them in shocked tones.

"I'm surprised you didn't see it somewhere on social media. His body was found in his car, and both were burned to a crisp."

They gasped and put their hands over their mouths.

"He'd been missing since New Year's Day. I think they found him on the third or fourth. Danae told me."

"Oh my God. That's terrible. I mean, Drake was an ass for cheating on you, but *damn!*" Braelynn said.

"Burned to a crisp. He ain't deserve all that." Myla added.

It took everything in me not to shout at the top of my lungs, *"Yes! He deserved every bit of pain he suffered and more! That nigga raped me!"* But I remained quiet.

I damn near shoved the pizza in my mouth to keep from

expressing my real feelings. However, my silence did not go unnoticed.

"Are you good, Jae? I know y'all had your ups and downs but —" Braelynn began.

"I'm good. Y'all ready to go?"

"In a minute. Let me—"

"I'm gonna go to the bathroom."

I got up before either of them could say anything else. I didn't want to talk about Drake, because I was glad the nigga was dead. I couldn't find an ounce of sympathy for him, and I refused to pretend. When I got to the bathroom, I actually did have to pee. After relieving my bladder, I stood at the sink, washing my hands. I heard the door swing open but didn't bother to see who it was. However, when I felt a presence near me, I looked to my right.

"Damn! Look at God! I prayed that one day I would see you again, and here you are," Vida said, with a satisfied smile.

Reaching for a paper towel, I dried my hands before speaking. "How can I help you?"

"You think you won, don't you?"

"I wasn't aware that there was a competition going on. Did I miss the memo?"

"I can't stand women like you. You had your chance with Kamden and didn't make a move until he moved on. Just couldn't stand to see him happy with someone else."

"If he was so happy with you, nothing I did would have convinced him to drop your ass. He ended it because he wanted to."

"No, he ended it because you lured him with the pussy you've been teasing him with for the past however long."

"Vida, believe what you want to believe. Kam told me about the ultimatum you gave him when he left you at the hotel. He still left, boo. Meaning, he made his choice. Deal with it."

I brushed past her, intentionally hitting her with my shoulder, then opened the door before throwing away the paper towel. When

I got back to the table, Braelynn and Myla were waiting for me, expectantly.

"What took you so long?

"You okay?"

"Yeah, I'm fine. Got a little visit from Vida," I told them.

"What?"

"Kam's ex?"

"Apparently, she wanted to get some shit off her chest," I told them.

At that moment, Vida walked by and went back to the booth where her friend was waiting. As soon as she sat down, she said something to her friend, and they both looked in our direction.

"Let's smile and wave," I suggested.

The three of us put big smiles on our faces and waved. Vida and her friend rolled their eyes and looked away.

"That was petty, but oh well." I shrugged my shoulders. "Y'all ready?"

"Yeah. We already paid the check." Myla informed me.

On the ride to Myla's house, I was expecting them to bring up Drake again, but thankfully, they left it alone.

"I did have some news that I've been waiting to share," Braelynn said.

"What?" we both said.

"I think I'm pregnant."

"What!" we repeated, this time with excitement.

"Yeah. I haven't taken a test yet, though. I'm kinda scared," she admitted.

"Why?"

"Because Kyree has been trying to get me pregnant for what seems like forever. Now that we are actively trying, I don't want him to be disappointed."

"You can take a test when we get to my house," Myla offered.

Braelynn took her eyes off the road for a quick second and looked at her while I stared at the back of her head.

"So you just got a stockpile of pregnancy tests at the crib?" Braelynn asked.

"Yep! Every month I think I'm pregnant. My husband refuses to wrap up and begged me not to get on birth control. We've been using spermicides and the sponge, but I'm never sure how well they work. Not to mention, we've had several slip-ups. So my ass be taking a test every other week," Myla explained.

"Damn, My," I said, shaking my head.

We pulled up at Myla's house, and when we got inside, Kolby looked like he was overjoyed to see us. He was sitting on the floor in the family room with the twins. Some of their toys were scattered all over the floor, and they were climbing all over him.

"Thank God, you're back. Your kids are on one today," he said as soon as he saw us.

"Oh, they're my kids now?" Myla replied with a grin.

"Baby, I tried to put them down for their nap, but their little asses wouldn't stop talking to each other through their damn cribs. It was like watching two inmates yelling through the bars in a jail cell," he complained.

"I told you it's time for us to put one of them in the other room. Come here, KJ and Mykha. Let's give daddy little break."

Neither of them were very stable on their feet yet, but Mykha had a little more balance than KJ. She made it halfway to Myla before she fell. KJ stood next to Kolby for a second, like he was thinking of a plan, then fell to his knees and crawled to his mother.

Kolby shook his head. "Your son is lazy, My. I'm gon' have to break him of that shit."

"He's not even one, Kolby. Stay off my nephew." Braelynn warned, picking him up.

"Wassup, y'all!" He finally greeted us. "I'm going downstairs to the office to do some work."

He kissed Myla and the twins before disappearing downstairs.

"Let me put them down before we do the you know what. I don't want any interruptions."

She took KJ from Braelynn and balanced both babies on her hips. I didn't know how the hell she handled both of their chubby asses.

Braelynn and I chilled in the family room while Myla put the kids down for a nap. I didn't know how long she was gone, but I fell asleep. I woke up to the two of them trying to whisper but failing miserably.

"Are y'all trying to whisper? If so, it's not working. Kolby probably heard every word."

"Come on. You can use the bathroom in the guest room," Myla said as they ignored my comment.

The three of us went to the guest room, and Myla and I waited for Braelynn to take the test.

"Shit, I'm nervous for her," I said.

"I was actually gonna suggest you take one, too, but it's too soon." Myla informed me.

"I wasn't about to take one anyway. I got enough on my mind."

Braelynn came out of the bathroom wearing a wide smile. It had only been about two minutes, but I assumed she got the results that she wanted.

"It only took thirty seconds to give me a positive. I'm pregnant, y'all!" she shouted, jumping up and down.

Myla and I hopped up and wrapped our arms around her as we congratulated her.

"Oh my God, sis! How do you feel?"

"I'm excited and nervous. How should I tell Kyree?"

"Well, don't do what I did." Myla joked, knowing damn well Braelynn wouldn't hide her pregnancy from Kyree for three whole months.

Braelynn rolled her eyes. "He probably already suspects it. I've missed two periods, but once we actively started trying, we agreed not to stress about it. The shop has been keeping us busy, which is probably why he hasn't asked."

"Two periods, Brae?" Myla asked. "You might be two months."

She nodded. "I've been taking prenatal vitamins for a couple of months, just in case."

"Are you trying to do something special to tell him or..." I asked.

"Honestly, I'm too excited to plan something special. I'll probably just make dinner and tell him tonight."

We hung out with Myla for a bit longer before heading to the grocery store, then to Braelynn's new house. This was my first visit since they'd moved in, and after giving me a tour, she went to start dinner.

I ended up taking a nap, and by the time I'd woken up, I decided to pop up on Kamden. Besides, I wanted to give Braelynn and Kyree some privacy. After a quick shower and throwing on some leggings and a hoodie, I exited the guest room.

"Hey, big bro!" I greeted Kyree when I stepped into the family room.

"Wassup, Jae. You good?"

"Yeah, I'm straight. About to pop up on your stubborn ass brother."

"Good luck with that."

"Hey, Brae. Can I use your truck?"

"Of course. The keys are by the door. Good luck," she said as she took something out of the oven.

When I arrived at Kamden's apartment about thirty minutes later, I hesitated before entering his building. I began to second-guess myself, thinking maybe I should have called first. I entered the second door and walked down the hall to his apartment. Just before I reached his door, it opened and I froze in place.

Kamden and Vida were in the doorway, and he pulled her into a hug and kissed her forehead.

"Thanks, Kamden. I appreciate your honesty," Vida said.

When they turned to face me, I saw a smirk on Vida's face while Kamden looked like he'd been caught with his hand in the cookie jar.

"Jae?"

I looked back and forth between the two of them, before putting all of my weight on one leg and folding my arms across my chest.

"Oh, so you do know who I am? What the fuck is this bitch doing here?"

"I got your bitch, *bitch*!" Vida took a step toward me, but Kamden got between us, facing me.

"V," he said, looking me directly in my eyes. "You need to go."

She stepped from behind him, and Kamden shifted his body so that he was still between us, but I was able to see her face.

With the same smirk on her face, she said, "We don't always choose wisely, Kam." Then she walked away.

KAMDEN

*J*aelynn and I remained in the hallway, facing off, well after Vida was gone. She still had her arms folded across her chest with her hip sticking out, wearing the sexiest mean mug I'd ever seen. Instead of arguing, which I knew we were about to do, I wanted to pull her into my arms and smother her mouth with mine. However, I was sure she would have tried to knock my ass out.

"We gon' stay out here staring at each other all night, or do you want to come inside so we can talk?"

Her eyes moved down to my chest and lingered at my dick print, which I knew was bulging because I had thoughts of fucking her in the hallway. When they made it back up to meet my eyes, I saw that hers were watery, but she refused to let a tear fall. *Mean ass!*

"Naw, I'm good on you. We ain't got shit to talk about."

She tried to walk around me, but of course, that shit wasn't about to happen.

"Kamden, move please."

"If you don't move your little ass into this apartment, we gon' be out here all night, baby girl."

After exhaling angrily, she pouted but went inside. I followed her, locked the door behind us, went to the living room, and sat on the couch. Jaelynn remained near the door. *Mean and stubborn ass!*

"Jae, come sit down."

I heard some rustling behind me, and when she sat across from me on the love seat, I saw that she'd taken off her boots and coat. She looked at me expectantly as she sat back, and just to fuck with her, I waited a while before I spoke up.

"She came over to talk about us... as in me and her. She needed closure."

"No, she came over here trying to shake up some shit. Did she tell you we ran into each other at Slice of Bronzeville today?"

The look of surprise on my face was all the answer she needed. *Why would Vida pop up over here after seeing Jaelynn? She must have had an ulterior motive.*

She leaned forward and rested her elbows on her thighs. "Didn't think so. That hoe knew I was in town and popped up over here trying to start some shit. Or... maybe she's the reason why you've been giving me your ass to kiss since you left Seattle."

"Jae, you know exactly why things are the way they are between us, and Vida coming over here ain't got a damn thing to do with it."

"You might as well add her being here to the list because I definitely have a problem with it."

Aggressively sitting back, she crossed one leg on top of the other, then did the same with her arms across her chest.

"Let's forget about Vida right now. We got more important shit we need to discuss," I told her.

"Oh, now you wanna talk? I've been trying to talk to your ass for two weeks, and you've been on mute!"

"I still don't wanna talk, but I'm ready to listen."

Minutes passed before she spoke again. I kept my eyes on her as

I patiently waited. Although I wanted to hear what she said, it didn't matter. I was still upset about the situation, but that didn't matter either. Jaelynn was *mine*, and when it was all said and done, we'd be together.

"Kam, I'm sorry, okay? I bought the Plan B because I thought you assumed that I was on birth control. I know you said that things didn't happen fast, but they did. That was a very emotional night, and neither of us was thinking."

"You may not have been thinking, but I knew exactly what I was doing."

"Oh, so you were trying to get me pregnant?"

"You know I want kids, Jae."

"I want kids, too, Kam."

"Then why would you even consider taking that shit?"

"Because I didn't have time to process whether or not I wanted to be giving birth nine months from now. Shit, Kam, I wasn't thinking. We've never talked about *us*, as in *me and you*, having kids. I'm sorry that I had a moment of uncertainty."

"Uncertainty? About us?"

"Yeah... I mean... no. Hell, I don't know. You had a girlfriend waiting for you in a hotel room. I didn't know—"

"Jae, I told you—"

"I know what you said, Kam, *after the fact*. Niggas say shit all the time."

I sat up. "I'm not just some random nigga!"

"I'm not saying you are. I'm saying I had a moment of uncertainty about what happened and what would happen in the immediate future. Showing up here and seeing you hugged up with her in the doorway makes me feel like my uncertainty was justified."

"Naw, we not gon' do that. Vida is not an issue. She never was. The moment you were ready to be mine, Vida, or any other woman, didn't exist to me. I was always gonna choose you, Jae. I was just waiting for you to choose me."

Silence filled the room again, and the one question I'd been wanting to ask her since I left her in Seattle, was on the tip of my tongue. I had to know.

"Did you take it?"

"No, I didn't take it."

More extended silence, although I felt a smile creep onto my lips.

"Thank you," I said softly.

"Why are you thanking me? I have no idea if I'm pregnant."

"I'm thanking you for being open to the possibility. Look, Jae, I'm sorry about the way that I reacted. You didn't make me wrap up, so I thought you were either on birth control, or were cool with whatever happening. Never did I consider you taking that pill after the fact. That shit caught me by surprise. I know I've been kinda distant with you, and I apologize for that, too. I needed a minute, but I admit, I could have handled this better."

"Yeah, you could have. Now, let's talk about Vida and why the fuck she was here."

I chuckled at her attempt at being tough. Before I replied, I stood and walked over to the love seat, then took up the space next to her. She tried to scoot over so that she wouldn't be touching me, but there was nowhere for her to go. Instead, she turned her body and put her elbow on the armrest, then rested her chin there, refusing to look in my direction.

"I missed the fuck outta you."

"Don't try to change the subject, Kam. Imagine you coming to Seattle and stopping by my house unexpectedly to find me hugged up with a nigga I used to fuck."

"Considering one of them is dead, I wouldn't recommend that shit."

That bold statement had her turning to look at me, eyes wide, mouth open, with a shocked expression. No, I didn't kill Drake, but if I had it my way, I would have. The fact remains, that nigga was dead.

When she didn't have a response, I continued. "Look, I know Vida being here seems suspicious."

"You think? You ain't got on shit but a pair of sweats that's barely keeping your dick in place, y'all were hugging, and you kissed her forehead."

"It was a goodbye hug and kiss!"

Her head whipped back around so quickly I was surprised she didn't have whiplash.

"Did you give her some goodbye dick, too? You know what? Fuck this!"

She tried to get up, but I pulled her back down and onto my lap before she had fully extended her legs into the standing position. Wrapping my arms around her body, limiting her movement, I pressed my forehead against hers.

"I didn't fuck her. I didn't want to fuck her. I love you, and my heart beats for you, and only you. You're the only one for me."

I used one of my hands to find the waistband of her leggings and panties. Dipping my hand inside, I quickly found her button and pressed my thumb against it. I slid my index and middle finger up and down her already-wet folds before pushing them inside her awaiting hole.

"Mmmm," she moaned.

"Just like your pussy only gets wet for me, my dick only gets hard for you. You're it for me, Jae. I already told you I waited a long time for you to be mine. You think I'm gon' do some shit to lose the person that means everything in this world to me?" I spoke to her while rubbing and stroking her to a climax. "Let that shit go, Jae." I encouraged, referring to the situation with Vida *and* her sticky juices that covered my fingers seconds later.

Carefully, I removed my fingers from her domain and lifted them to my mouth, licking them clean. Still on my lap, eyes closed, and breathing hard, a smile crept onto her lips.

"Why you smiling?"

"Because I missed your ass, too," she confessed as she tried to catch her breath.

I finally was able to smother her lips with mine, and we spent the rest of the night making up for lost time.

JAELYNN

When Myla said that Kolby was doing the most for the twins' birthday party, she didn't exaggerate one bit. I thought the baby shower was over the top, but it was nothing compared to KJ and Mykha's party.

They'd rented the same space they used for the baby shower, and the theme was "Frolic on the Farm with KJ and Mykha". Erica, of Evolving Diva Inc. Events, the event planner that they'd hired for their baby shower, was also hired for the twins' party. She had that place looking like the twins were the children of celebrities.

The week before the party, when I wasn't with Kamden or we weren't working on details for our upcoming fashion show, I was helping Myla get ready for the twins' party. Although the party was catered and the event planner took care of almost everything, Myla had to make sure the four of them had matching outfits and a few other minor details. *Whatever happened to kids having birthday parties at McDonald's?*

KJ and Mykha behaved like typical one-year-olds. They were whiny, attached to their parents, and afraid of all the animals. Other than that, the party was a huge success. *I guess.*

The immediate family had all come back to Myla and Kolby's house to hang out for a little while. Ms. Stella had been trying to get me alone all day. I hadn't seen her since we were in Belize for the wedding. She finally cornered me in the kitchen.

"You look happy," she said, hugging me.

"I am happy. I don't think I've ever been happier."

"I've never seen Kamden this happy. For the past year or so, the boy would be angry sometimes for no damn reason. Those were the times when I knew not being with you the way he wanted was wearing on him."

"It didn't seem like it bothered him that much. He never directed his anger my way."

"Remember when I told you that Kamden was my most passionate son?"

I nodded.

"Well, he's also the most impatient. I couldn't believe the amount of patience he had with you. That let me know how much he loves and respects you. It was very hard for him to not have you the way he wanted."

"It was hard for me, too. Honestly, I was miserable, but I wanted to be whole before I gave him my heart. I'm still working on myself, but being with Kamden... he makes me feel whole. His love is healing my heart in ways that I didn't think were possible."

"And you've only been together a few weeks. *Imagine that!*" she said that last part with a lot of sass.

"Even his friendship was healing, though. It just wasn't enough." I laughed.

"Well, I'm not sure what all happened for you two to come together. I'm just glad it happened."

"Me, too."

We hugged and she went on her way while I tried to remember why I came in the kitchen in the first place.

Delilah, Myla's mom, and Myles were in town. Auntie Dee had

already gone to bed. My mom was in town as well and was staying with Braelynn and Kyree. When she found out that Braelynn was pregnant, I thought she would never stop crying. It was going to be hard to get her to go back to Seattle. She is over the moon excited about her first grandbaby. Mr. Isaac and Ms. Stella left not long after our talk.

The TV in the family room was on Spotify. A mixture of today's R&B and hip-hop was playing in the background, and everyone was booed up except for Myles. I was surprised that he hadn't found something, or someone, to get into. I guess the night was still young. He'd been to Chicago enough times at this point that he didn't need the Ross brothers as a guide. Myla had just put the twins to bed and rejoined us in the family room.

"Damn, baby sis! I still can't believe your ass is married with two kids. You really grew up on a nigga," Myles commented before sipping the beer in his hand.

"Sometimes, I can't believe it either. And your brother-in-law stay trying to get me pregnant again. I'm barely handling the two we have," she responded as Kolby pulled her onto his lap.

"You handle motherhood like a G, baby. That's why I can't wait to plant a few more seeds," Kolby said, kissing her cheek.

Myles frowned up his face. "I know you grown, but I don't wanna hear that shit. You still my baby."

Everyone laughed, and Myles continued. "Hell, all three of y'all my babies. I heard you out here being grown, too, Brae. Congratulations!"

"Thanks, bro," Braelynn replied.

"We just trying to keep up with Kolby and Myla. They already got the two-for-one deal," Kyree added while his sister-in-law rolled her eyes.

"We waiting on you to settle down and give us a niece or nephew." Braelynn added.

Myles was shaking his head before she even finished the statement. "Naw, I can't even see that happening any time soon. Especially a kid." He shook his head again. "These women out here too damn crazy to carry my seeds."

"I know one that you'd be trying to trap if she gave you a second chance." Myla teased.

He looked at Myla, and although he had a smile on his face, we could see the sadness in his eyes. In his mid-twenties, Myles lost his one true love because he didn't want to leave the streets. He hadn't been in a serious relationship since then, and that was ten years ago.

"Who? Ev?" Myla nodded. "That ship sailed a long time ago. Last I heard, she was engaged." The hurt could be heard in his voice, but he would never admit to it. Everleigh Noble was the love of his life.

"She might be, but that doesn't mean you wouldn't jump at a second chance with her."

"Whatever, sis. Enough about me. I don't need to have no damn kids with the way y'all spittin' them out around here. You're next, Jae."

"Yep!" Kamden said, confidently. He then had the nerve to rub my stomach, and I pushed him on the shoulder.

"Boy, be quiet! Myles, I am not pregnant."

We were still out here being reckless, so there was a chance that Kamden was right, but I didn't want us to get ahead of ourselves.

"You got a real one right there, Jae. He definitely got my vote," Myles offered, giving Kamden a look that only the two of them understood.

Although nobody understood the look, we all saw it. Everyone looked between Myles and Kamden, and Kyree spoke up.

"Why do I feel like there's something we missed?" he asked.

"It's not my story to tell, but the youngin' got some real heart," Myles replied. "Jae, he may fuck up, because all men do at some point, but always remember, he was willing to go the extra mile for you."

"You talking in code, bruh. One of y'all niggas need to speak up. Kamden, you know we don't keep real shit from each other," Kyree said, suddenly in big brother mode.

"This ain't the time to have this conversation. Not in front of them," Kamden said, referring to me, Braelynn, and Myla.

"Why not? I—" I began, but Kamden cut me off.

"Jaelynn!" he said with authority.

His tone combined with the look on his face should have been enough to shut me up. But I wanted to know what happened, and now was my chance.

"Why can't you tell me what happened?" I pressed.

He leaned in and whispered in my ear, "Baby girl, if we open up this can of worms, you have to tell them everything. If you're not ready to do that, leave it alone." He pulled back and looked at me, waiting for a reply.

Was my curiosity strong enough for me to share my deepest and darkest secret? Did I really need to know?

I'd never planned on sharing it with anyone, but since I'd shared it with Kamden and started therapy, I felt much lighter. I knew that the people in that room loved and supported me. *It was time.*

"I'm ready," I told him.

"Are you sure? You don't—"

"It's time, Kam."

He nodded and kissed my temple. Six pairs of eyes were on me, but I didn't feel nervous. I almost felt ...relieved.

"Myla, do you remember, after Drake and I broke up, we went to that event and ran into him?"

"Yeah. He acted a complete asshole."

"When I got home, he was waiting for me. I let myself in and tried to close the door in his face, but he forced his way in. We, umm... we argued, and he..." I wiped away the tears that had fallen and looked at Braelynn and Myla.

The tears were already falling from their eyes, as if they know what I was about to say. My eyes went to the angry faces of their husbands, then to Myles. They all looked like they were doing their best to keep their composure.

"You good?" Kamden asked as he softly rubbed his hand up and down my back.

I nodded. "He raped me."

Braelynn and Myla released a wail that I could feel, then rushed to my side. Kamden moved, allowing them space to console me.

"Jae, why didn't you tell us? Why didn't you go to the police? Does Ma know?"

Both of them, through their tears, had many questions. I answered them as best I could. For many of them, I didn't have the answers, but most of them I could have answered with one word... fear. Fear stopped me from speaking up and from living my life for far too long.

"Ma doesn't know, and I don't want her to ever know. It would break her heart."

They both nodded in understanding.

Braelynn must have connected some dots because suddenly, her expression changed, and she asked in an elevated tone, "Kamden, did you kill Drake?"

"Kill?"

"Hold up."

Kyree and Kolby were caught by surprise with that question.

"You said you beat his ass. You ain't say shit about killing," Kyree said.

"I hadn't gotten there yet," Kamden explained.

Apparently, while my sisters comforted me, Kamden and Myles were telling Kyree and Kolby what I'd been waiting to hear.

"You killed somebody?" Kolby shouted.

"Naw, nigga. He ain't kill nobody. Lower your damn voice." Myles warned.

"Aye, y'all ain't telling this shit fast enough. Don't nobody say another word until we hear all this shit," Kyree spat.

Kamden then told everything, beginning at the club on New Year's Eve, ending at the warehouse that Myles took him to, where he said he beat the shit out of Drake. A wave of relief took over my body when he added, "But he was still breathing when we left."

Kamden gave Myles a look that I couldn't read, but Myles had nothing to say about the situation, and we knew not to ask. Even if Myles didn't do it himself, he knew exactly what happened to Drake. What we knew now was all we'd ever know.

KAMDEN

"I can't believe I'm doing this shit!" I complained to my brothers.

"Me either. Braelynn didn't trip like this."

"Shit, Myla would have. The first thing she asked me when we went to my bedroom was, 'is this where you bring all your women to snatch their souls?'"

"You lying, bruh," Kyree said, laughing hard.

"Not at all. I would have been doing just like Kam and getting rid of a perfectly good mattress—"

"And pillows?" I added.

"And pillows. Myla was not about to sleep anywhere that I'd had sex with another woman."

"Didn't you just get this mattress? You don't even bring women to the crib. It can't be that used."

"Six months ago, and the only woman that's ever been here is Vida. Hell, now that I think about it, that's probably why she's making me do this."

We'd finally gotten my "old" king-sized mattress outside, which

I was certain someone would get off the curb before long. The new mattress should be delivered within the hour.

"You should have just told her you got a new one. How would she have known?" Kyree said.

"Because she made me go with her to pick one out."

We sat around my apartment, catching up, while we waited for the mattress to be delivered. Although we'd talked, the last time we'd seen each other was the previous weekend at Kolby's house, after the twins' birthday party.

"How is Jae? How is she dealing with the rape?" Kolby asked.

"She started therapy, and she says it's helping. Even since she's been here, she's had a few appointments through video conferencing. She seems to be handling it better. You have to remember, this happened two years ago. She dealt with it alone for a long time. I think she buried it and tried not to think about it as best she could. The fact that the nigga is dead does give her some level of comfort, but it doesn't take away what happened."

"Damn, man! I'm glad his blood ain't on your hands, but I don't know how you stopped yourself from taking his life," Kyree commented.

"I ain't gon' lie. I went there fully expecting to kill that nigga. He was barely breathing when Myles had one of his boys pull me away from him. He didn't want his blood on my hands either. When we left, I asked him why he didn't let me end him. He said his people end lives regularly and sleep well at night."

"Shit! I thought Myla said he was trying to get outta that life," Kyree said.

"Yeah, but how does that even work?"

The three of us laughed because we didn't know shit about the kind of lifestyle that Myles lived. Growing up, our parents kept a tight hold on us and made sure we stayed on the straight and narrow. We got in a fair amount of trouble, but it was regular shit, nothing too serious.

We talked a little longer, but they left when the mattress was delivered. Jaelynn and I had been sleeping in Kolby's old room. I guess she didn't have an issue with sleeping where her sister and my brother had sex. *Silly ass girl!*

Several hours later, I was fresh out of the shower, with my dick and nuts clean and hanging free. The new mattress was on the bed, adorned with the new sheet and comforter set that Jaelynn insisted I get. I'd ordered some food from the Chinese restaurant around the corner and was waiting for it to be delivered. Smooth old-school R&B set the atmosphere through the surround sound speakers. All I needed was baby girl to bring her ass home, and she'd just let me know that she was on the way.

I heard a knock on the door and knew it was the food. Since I used DoorDash, all I had to do was grab it from the delivery person. Once I did that, I washed my hands and prepped the food. Not long after, I heard keys in the door, and Jaelynn walked in.

"Hey, baby girl." I greeted as I approached her.

"What's all this?" she asked, looking around as she took off her coat, then hung it on the coatrack.

I had the lights dimmed and candles lit throughout the apartment while Boyz II Men serenaded us with "I'll Make Love to You".

"Nothing much. Just a little dinner and music."

"Aww, Kam." She lifted to her toes for a quick kiss, then put her arms around my waist. "This is sweet. Wait... you didn't cook, did you?"

"Jae, it's common knowledge that the Ross brothers can do everything, except cook. This is from the Chinese food place around the corner."

"Just making sure you ain't trying to kill me."

I kissed her forehead, nose, and lips before saying, "I am gon' kill that pussy a little later, but first, let's eat."

"Whatever, nasty! I'm gonna take a quick shower," she said, before heading down the hall to the guest bedroom where all of her things were.

While she did that, I finished plating our food and poured us some good old-fashioned grape Kool-Aid. When she returned, wearing a T-shirt and a tiny pair of terry cloth shorts, I had to talk my dick down. This might be the quickest dinner in history. Once she was seated, I heated her food for a quick minute before serving her, then did the same to mine. When I sat down, we held hands, and I blessed the food before we dug in.

"How was your day?" she asked.

"Straight. I'm happy that I can sleep in my own room now."

"The mattress came today?"

I nodded.

"How does the new comforter set look?"

I shrugged. "Like a comforter set. How was your day?"

"Busy as hell, but we were able to choose all of our models for the show. We'll have rehearsal three times next week and every day the following week, leading up to the show. This is a lot more work than we anticipated, but I think it's gonna turn out really well."

"Y'all gon' kill it, and I'll be front and center to watch it all unfold."

"Umm, maybe you should support me from afar. I don't know if I want you front and center drooling all over half-naked women."

"Why? The only woman I've ever drooled over is you."

"I'm kidding. You know, I really want to start this men's line soon," she said, changing the subject.

"What are you waiting for?"

"Time, I guess. There's been so much going on since—shit, since we met y'all, honestly. Now that things are beginning to settle down, I can focus on that a little more."

"The Ross brothers came on the scene and rocked y'all worlds, huh?"

She rolled her eyes but couldn't hide her grin.

When she didn't reply, I said, "Speaking of rocking worlds... how long do we have to wait before you take a test?"

Her beautiful face went into a frown. "A test for what?"

"A pregnancy test."

"Oh." Her face softened. "I'm not sure. My last period was... oh shit!" She let her fork fall to her plate. "It started a few days before Christmas. I'm late."

"Late, as in you might be pregnant, late?"

"I don't know. I've never been late before. It could be stress."

"Or you could be pregnant."

"Possibly."

"Take a test."

She shook her head while saying, "Not yet. Let's wait a little longer."

"How long?"

"I don't know. Maybe a couple of weeks."

"That long?"

"It'll fly by. Please, babe, can we wait?"

I didn't want to, but I agreed. I was pretty confident that she was pregnant anyway. I just wanted her to take the test for confirmation.

We finished our dinner and cleaned up the kitchen together. Once that was done, we went to the living room and got comfortable on the couch. My body was extended the length of the couch, and Jaelynn positioned herself between my legs, with her back against my chest. I picked up the remote and was about to turn off Spotify, but Jaelynn stopped me.

"No, I wanna sit here, chill, listen to music, and talk."

Putting the remote down, I snaked my arms through hers, rested my hands on her stomach, then kissed her temple before replying with, "Okay. What do you want to talk about?"

"A couple of days after the fashion show, I'm going back to Seattle. How are we handling this?"

I thought about how my brothers navigated through their long-distance relationships, and I now understood why they were short-lived. It took Braelynn about seven months to move to Chicago, and Myla about four. There was no doubt that I wanted Jaelynn with me permanently within three months, although I hadn't shared that with her yet.

"I've waited almost two years for moments like this. To be able to lay up with you, to hold you in my arms, to dig deep in that pussy."

She kissed her teeth and nudged my side with her elbow.

"Shit, it's true." I continued. "I feel like we've been in a long-distance relationship all this time. You're the first woman I've ever loved, and it was hard being your friend because I wanted to be your man. But now that you're mine, I appreciate our friendship. We don't have to go through that awkward stage of getting to know each other, because we already know everything about each other. I wasn't playing when I told you that we could get married right now. I want you with me every day."

"I want to be with you every day, too."

"I guess we need to get you moved."

"I guess so."

The sweet sounds of Zhané's "Sweet Taste of Love" now played through the speakers. We sat quietly, enjoying each other. My hands moved from her stomach to the waistband of her shorts. When I felt her bare pussy, my dick jumped. I slid two of my fingers down her slit and groaned when I felt how slick she already was. I pressed my thumb against her clit and pushed my fingers inside her beckoning hole.

"Hmm, shit," she whispered.

Taking my free hand, I gently pulled her head to the side, giving me more access to her neck, then kissed it softly at first before sucking hard enough to leave my mark. Her legs opened wider as I used my fingers and thumb to pleasure her. The more I stroked, the wetter she got. My dick was hard as hell pressed against her back.

"Mmmm," she moaned. "Fuck, I'm cummin'."

Her legs suddenly tightened around my hand, and I could feel the walls of her pussy pulsing around my fingers. When she reached the top of her climax, she screamed my name, making me wish it was my dick instead of my hand inside of her. I pulled my fingers from her sweetness and put one of them into my mouth, savoring the goodness.

"Open up," I told her.

She obeyed my command, and I dipped the other finger into her mouth, letting her taste the goodness that she had between her thighs. Once she was completely recovered, she sat up and maneuvered her body so that she was on her knees, between my legs, facing me.

Her tiny hand went to the massive bulge between my legs. The head was sticking out of the top of my sweats, and precum had oozed onto my stomach. She pulled down the waistband, and my dick popped up. Positioning herself perfectly, she used one hand to brace herself while the other gripped the base of my dick.

When her tongue touched the tip, then swirled around, licking away my anxious fluid, it felt like heaven. She did that a few times before covering the whole head with her mouth. After gently sucking on it, like it was her favorite lollipop, the head suddenly hit the back of her throat.

"Fuck!" I groaned.

Baby girl's head game had me wanting to pick out a ring tomorrow morning. The moisture in her mouth began to build, allowing it to smoothly glide up and down my length. When she started to apply some suction, I almost lost my goddamn mind.

"Shit, Jae!"

My hand went into her head, and I proceeded to uncontrollably fuck her mouth. Jae's gag reflex was non-fucking-existent.

"I'm about to blow!" I warned, and before I said "blow", my seeds shot down her throat. "Arghhhh!"

Jae kept sucking until I was empty, causing my dick to stay hard. When I pulled her head away, she swallowed with a smile on her face.

"Take those fuckin' shorts off and sit on this shit!" I demanded, then thought better of it. "Naw, fuck that. Move that shit to the side."

She did as she was told and sank onto my dick. Every time I entered her, it felt like home. Nobody, not even God, could tell me that Jaelynn wasn't made for me. It was like every day that we spent trying to be just friends, my feelings for her grew tenfold.

"Ride that shit, Jae." I encouraged, slapping her ass.

I gripped the back of her neck and pulled her face to mine, sucking on her bottom lip before kissing her deeply. She continued to wind her hips on my dick, and when she tore her mouth away from mine and sat up, I knew her climax was near.

"Kam, shit!" she moaned as her hands went to my chest.

"Shit, yeah! Ride yo' dick, baby girl."

Using my chest to balance herself, she bounced up and down on my shit, and I felt my nut rising a lot faster than I wanted it to. I held onto her hips to control her movements, slowing her pace.

"Mmm, Kam. Let me go! I'm about to cum!"

"Fuck it then. Me too!"

I released her hips and let her do her thing. Seconds later, our orgasms collided, and our voices filled the room with expletives. Joining Janet Jackson as "That's the Way Love Goes" brought us down from our high.

JAELYNN

The last couple of weeks had been crazy as hell. The amount of preparation that went into a fashion show was unreal. Braelynn, Myla, and I had been working our asses off trying to make sure it was a success. Dealing with so many personalities was not easy, and there were times when we wanted to give up. However, the day had arrived, and there was no turning back.

The start time was seven p.m., and the models' arrival time to begin getting ready was three. The three of us arrived at one o'clock and were in the process of getting each piece of lingerie organized for each scene. Although I cut it *extremely* close, I ended up designing a few pairs of pajama and lounge bottoms for men. Thankfully, a few of our female models knew some fine ass men that were willing to participate in the show.

Time flew by, and the models started to arrive. From the outside looking in, it probably looked like chaos, but things were actually going smoothly. Braelynn had been experiencing morning sickness for the last two weeks. She'd recently made it to her second trimester, hitting fourteen weeks. And so far, she hadn't been sick today.

Our mothers flew in and, along with Ms. Stella, were on hand to help. It was already an hour before showtime, and the three of us still had to make ourselves presentable. We came across this young DJ by the name of DJ Fly Ty, and he had the guests rocking while they waited for the show to start. He was only seventeen and was playing music from every genre and decade. He was truly dope!

"I can't believe we have less than an hour before the show starts," Braelynn said. "I'm so fuckin' excited."

"Me too!" Myla and I said simultaneously.

"Did one of y'all get a chance to peek out there? It's already packed."

"I did, and I thought seeing all those people would make me nervous, but it calmed me," I said.

"There's no turning back now. This is about to happen. No need to be nervous," Myla said.

"True!" Braelynn and I agreed.

We continued to chat while we finished getting ready. We were all wearing ripped jeans with a pair of over-the-knee boots. Since the color scheme of MyLynn's Bedroom Boutique was red, black, and gray, I wore red boots, Braelynn wore a black pair, and Myla's were gray.

We had custom made blinged-out T-shirts made with our company name in the same colors, and our shirt matched our boots. We didn't want to be too dressed up because we knew we'd be behind the scenes working until the end of the show, but we did want to be cute.

"Fifteen minutes until showtime," Ma said when she stuck her head in the room. "And there are some handsome gentlemen out here that want to see you. Can I send them in?"

"Yeah!" we all said.

The Ross brothers walked into the room, looking like they were about to grace the runway. Kyree and Kolby went to their wives, and Kamden came to me.

"Hey, baby girl. You ready?" He greeted after kissing my forehead, nose, and lips.

"I am. How does it look out there?"

"The only empty seats are ours. Y'all gon' be the talk of the city."

"I doubt it. Chicago is a big city, but I'm glad it's packed. Our tickets sold out. It's just crazy to see it."

"I love you, and I'm proud of you."

"Thank you, babe. I love you, too."

They left to take their seats after wishing us all luck, and it was time for the show to begin.

WE WERE DOWN to the last scene, which we named "Wedding Night", and everything had gone off without a hitch. I didn't think we could have asked for a better show. Then it happened. Our model for the last scene became suddenly ill. She was nauseous and lightheaded and didn't think she could make it down the runway and back. This particular model was very petite, with small breasts, a small waist, and a nice handful of ass. Kind of like...

"Jaelynn, you have to do it. You and Kiara are built the exact same way," Myla urged.

"What? Are you crazy? I'm not a model."

"I would do it, but now, I have a pooch," Braelynn said, patting her baby bump.

"Are y'all for real?"

"Yes! And we don't have time to go back and forth," came from Myla.

I knew I had to do it. Kiara was the only model we had with her build because we had ladies of various shapes and sizes.

"Come on, Jae. We don't have much time. You're gonna need a little more makeup now, too." Braelynn pressed.

Begrudgingly, I sat in the chair, and one of the makeup artists we hired worked quickly applying my makeup. Braelynn wet my hair with a spray bottle to add a bit more life to my curls. Finally, I went behind the curtain and put on the white, one-piece, lace lingerie.

The ass was lace and cupped my small but plump one perfectly. The back material was cut out in the shape of a heart. My small breasts were covered, but my stomach was exposed because another piece of missing heart-shaped material. Thankfully, it came with a white sheer robe. When I came from behind the curtain, Myla and Braelynn gasped.

"Okay, umm. Just go down, take off the robe, face the left, then the right, do a little turn, then come back... if Kamden doesn't yank your ass off the stage."

My eyes got big. I'd forgotten about Kamden.

"Oh my God! Are y'all heffas trying to get me killed?"

"It's too late to think about that now, but we won't let him kill you, though."

These bitches!

I slipped on a pair of silver heels, wishing they weren't my size so I could have a reason to back out. Then I heard the MC's voice.

"Are y'all ready for the finale?" she said.

The crowd responded with claps and cheers.

"Next up, we have... hold on, there was a quick change in models. We have Jaelynn Waters, one-third of MyLynn's Bedroom Boutique, filling in for Kiara."

"You got this, sis!" Braelynn whispered.

"Marry Me" by Jason Derulo began to play, and I looked at my girls in confusion because that wasn't the song we had chosen. They shrugged their shoulders and shooed me along. *These hoes!*

I rolled my eyes at them before stepping to the stage that led to the runway. Taking a deep breath, I put on my best unbothered look and began my sexy strut. It definitely wasn't the model walk, but I was on tempo with the music. I knew the vicinity of where Kamden was seated, and I refused to look in his direction. If he jumped on stage and snatched me off, then so be it. My ass didn't belong up there anyway. The light was so bright, I couldn't see anyone's faces, but I could hear murmurs in the crowd. I wasn't sure if that was good or bad.

By the time I reached the end of the runway, I took the sheer robe off and swung it over my shoulder, turned to the left, then right, then a full turn, before headed back down the runway. Halfway down the runway, I saw Kamden enter the stage and head in my direction. My reaction was to stop moving because I didn't know what the hell was going on.

When Kamden reached me, the smile he wore was contagious, and although I was confused, I smiled as well.

"Baby, what are you—"

Before I could finish my question, he was down on one knee. Jason Derulo's voice faded out, and Kamden pulled a microphone from his back pocket and held it in one hand; a ring box appeared in the other. My hand went over my mouth, and tears filled my eyes.

"Jaelynn Michaela Waters, you are my best friend, my heart, and my soul. I love you with all that is in me, and I want to spend the rest of my life showering you with that love. I feel like I've been waiting my whole life, to ask you this... Will you do me the honor of being my wife?"

"God, yes! Yes, yes, yes, I will be your wife!"

He dropped the mic and opened the ring box. I didn't know a damn thing about diamonds, but it was a square cut and a nice size. He slid it onto my finger, and it fit perfectly. When he stood to his feet, he wrapped me in his arms and planted a kiss on my lips that was so powerful that I felt lightheaded. The crowd roared around us, but it felt like we were alone. In this moment, our love was all that mattered.

KAMDEN

The video ofme proposing to Jaelynn went viral. We had to turn off our Instagram and Facebook notifications because they were driving us crazy, almost to the point of deleting the apps, but we couldn't for business purposes. Someone from Windy City Live, the Chicago-based morning talk show, contacted us about coming on the show, but neither of us was interested. The viral video was already more attention than we wanted.

Jaelynn's flight left early this morning. I tried to talk her into moving her flight back a couple of days, but her stubborn ass wanted to go home to start packing, so I couldn't be mad about that. I would have gone to Seattle with her, but one of my cleaning crews was starting at a new building today. Whenever I got a new contract, I liked to work with the crew for the first couple of days to make sure they were off to a good start. I'd be flying out there in a couple of days.

With the excitement of the engagement, I fucked around and forgot all about her taking a pregnancy test. As soon as I touch down in Seattle in a couple of days, I was going to the pharmacy to pick one up. I had a strong feeling that she was pregnant because her period still hadn't made an appearance.

Kolby had connected me with his realtor, Vic Swanson, and I was meeting him at his office. Since Jaelynn and I were getting married and hopefully having a baby soon, it was time to find a house. Today, I would be filling out all of the necessary paperwork to get qualified, and when Jaelynn and I returned to Chicago, Vic would have a few houses lined up to show us.

Vic's office was at the end of a strip mall. It had snowed the night before, and the parking lot was a slushy mess. I'd just left work and thankfully, was still wearing my work boots.

As I approached the door, I heard someone calling my name. I looked around, and because it was already dark outside, I didn't realize that the bundled-up woman coming toward me was Vida until she was standing in front of me.

"Hey," she said when she was in front of me.

"Wassup?"

"Nothing. I was going into TJ Maxx and saw your car drive by. Just wanted to say hi."

"Hi."

"I saw the video of your proposal. Congratulations," she said, without an ounce of feeling.

"Thank you. Look, I have an appointment that I don't want to be late for. It was good to see you."

"You're buying a house already? Moving kinda fast, aren't you?"

I had pulled the door partially open and paused, releasing a deep breath.

"Vida, do you need something? Because this conversation is a waste of time."

"Oh, now I'm a waste of time? You know what, Kamden? Fuck you!"

She turned and tried to stomp away, but the slippery sidewalk didn't allow her to make a grand exit. I shook my head and went inside the realtor's office. Vic was coming out of his office.

"Hey, Kamden. It's good to see you again." Vic greeted.

Vic was one of Kolby's friends in high school, and they remained cool. I'd seen him a few times recently since he and Kolby had reconnected. He helped both my brothers find homes, so I was hoping he could do the same for me.

"Good to see you, too."

"Well, let's go ahead and get started. If you have all of the necessary paperwork that I requested, this shouldn't take very long."

"Cool."

I followed him into his office and took a seat in front of his desk, then set the envelope with the paperwork he requested on top.

"I saw the proposal on Facebook. That was pretty smooth. Congratulations!"

"Thank you! It was actually a last-minute thing. Braelynn and Myla actually came up with the idea when I told them I wanted to propose."

"People are eating it up. When I saw it, there were over a million views."

"Really? That's crazy. I turned off my notifications, so I haven't seen it since Sunday."

"Oh, yeah! I bet your phones were going crazy."

He picked up the envelope and sorted through what I brought. There was a tap on his office door, causing us to look in that direction.

"What's up, Clark?" Vic asked his coworker.

"Umm, you guys may wanna come see this. Especially you." He directed to me.

I looked at Vic, and we both got up and followed Clark to the front door. We looked through the windows, and because it was dark outside, it took me a second to comprehend what I was seeing.

"Is that your truck?" Clark asked.

"What the fuck?" I pushed through the door and jogged to my car, the slush almost caused me to fall on my ass.

I grabbed the crowbar from Vida's hand mid-swing and tossed it to the side. This bitch had busted out all my damn windows and slashed my tires.

"Bitch! Are you fuckin' crazy?"

My mother would *kill* me if she knew I called a woman a bitch, but I was *pissed*. I turned her around roughly and pushed her against the truck. Remaining in front of her, I blocked her from moving. Her chest heaved up and down as she struggled against me.

"What the hell is wrong with you?"

"You broke my heart and expect me to just move on!"

"I apologized for that shit, and you said you were over it. What the fuck do you want from me?"

"I want you! You didn't even give us a chance," she cried.

"You thought fuckin' up my car was gon' get you a chance? Get the—"

"Sir! Stand back and put your hands up!" I heard behind me.

I was so pissed off that I didn't even see the police lights. Slowly, I took a few steps away from Vida, put my hands up, and turned toward the officer. He had his gun drawn and aimed at a nigga.

"Officer, he's not—" Vic approached and began to explain. He put his hands up and took a few steps back.

"Stand back!" I heard from someone who I assumed was another officer.

I couldn't see the owner of the voice because there was a van blocking my view. I didn't know who the fuck called the police, but I knew the shit wasn't gonna end in my favor.

JAELYNN

My flight back to Seattle was early. Coincidentally, my mom was on the same flight. Auntie Dee, Myla's mom, was staying for a few more days. When we landed, all I wanted to do was eat and take a nap. I was glad I parked my car at the airport this time instead of taking an Uber. My mom talked me into hanging out at her house for a bit, so we stopped and got something to eat and took it to her house.

While we ate, we caught up with each other. She'd been trying to talk to me since Kamden and I picked her up from Braelynn's house on the way to the airport. I was too damn tired for conversation. Kamden had me face down, ass up all damn night. I swear the nigga was insatiable. He was so focused on getting his fill of my pussy before I left that he didn't remind me to take a pregnancy test. There was really no need because I knew I was.

"Didn't I tell you those Ross brothers don't play? Have you thought about a wedding date yet?"

"One sec, Ma. This is Kam FaceTiming me. Hey, babe. My bad, I forgot to tell you we landed."

"It's cool, baby girl. Everything good?" he replied.

"Yeah. We picked up some food and are at my mom's house. I'm gonna hang out here for a while."

"Okay. Call me when you get home. I love you."

"Love you, too."

I ended the call to find my mom staring at me, smiling.

"What?"

"Nothing. Didn't I tell you those Ross brothers don't play? Have you thought about a wedding date yet?" she repeated.

"It's only been a few days, Ma."

"That don't mean a thing. Kamden ain't gon' wait too long. I'm sure he wants to be married like yesterday."

"We haven't talked about the wedding yet, but... I think I'm pregnant."

She gasped and put her hand over her mouth for a moment. "Already? Jaelynn!"

"I know, Ma. I haven't taken a test yet, but my period is a few weeks late. Everything with Kamden has been moving so fast, although he disagrees."

"Is it moving too fast for *you*?"

"I'm the happiest I've ever been, Ma. I am nervous about being somebody else's mama, though."

"You're gonna be a great mama. I mean, you've had a great example." She smiled and pointed to herself.

"I sure have." I smiled back, reached across and squeezed her hand. "He wants me move as soon as possible and even joked about you moving to Chicago."

"With both of my babies and my grandbabies there, he's right. I've been thinking about it since Brae told me she was pregnant. With your father gone, maybe it's time for a change."

We sat in silence for a minute. My thoughts were on my father, and I was sure hers were as well. I wondered if he would like Kamden and what kind of grandfather he would be. It had been almost five years since he passed away, and I missed him so much.

"Having you in Chicago with us would make everything

perfect, Ma. I can't believe Braelynn is so far along already. She probably got pregnant in Belize."

We talked for a while, until I began to yawn.

"Ma, I need a nap."

"You going home or to your room?"

"I think I'll go to my room."

After throwing away my trash, I gave my mom a hug, then went and had the best nap ever.

When I woke up, it was getting dark outside. I must have slept for a long time. My mom was in the living room watching one of her shows. She'd already showered and in her pajamas.

"You must have been tired. I had to come in there to check and see if you were still breathing."

"I was exhausted. What are you watching?"

"You know, I don't even know. I was flipping through, and it looked interesting."

I laughed. "Well, I'm gonna head home."

She got up from the recliner and gave me a hug. I kissed her cheek.

"Love you, sweetheart. Text me when you make it in."

"Love you more, Ma."

She saw me to the door, and I hopped in my car to head home. Before I pulled away from her house, I took my 9mm out of the glove compartment and put it in my purse. I'd been a little less paranoid since I didn't have to worry about Drake, but he wasn't the only crazy person in the world.

I stopped by a Walgreens to pick up a pregnancy test and a few other random things, then went to Chick-fil-A to get something for dinner. By the time I got to my house, it was dark. I put my purse across my body and grabbed my bags. Going to the trunk, I retrieved my suitcase and headed to my front door.

"Jaebaby!" I heard a deep voice yell, and I froze momentarily.

Without turning around, I let go of my suitcase and stuck my hand in my purse to grip my gun. Before I could take another step, the person who owned that deep voice was right behind me. He grabbed the hood of my coat and yanked me back. I dropped the bags I was holding, but my hand was still on my gun.

"I never could stand your bougie ass!" Drew said through gritted teeth. He still had a grip on my hood and was standing behind me, with his mouth close to my ear.

"Drew, please let me go!"

"You picked the wrong brother, Jaebaby. He's not here to protect your pretty ass. It's time for me to sample the goods."

His free hand went around my neck, and he squeezed as he said, "Don't make this harder on yourself."

I put my free hand on top of his and tried to pull it away from my neck, but he was too strong. "Get—the fuck—off—me."

When Drew slammed me to the ground and punched me in my face, it stunned me, but it didn't stop me from pulling my 9mm from my purse. I aimed and pulled the trigger.

"Bitch! I should kill your ass."

I think I got him in the shoulder, but clearly, it didn't hurt him enough. When he came toward me, I pulled the trigger two more times, hitting him in the chest. He managed to kick me on the side of my stomach before he fell on top of me.

"You bitch."

"Help me! Somebody help me!" I screamed as I tried to push Drew's body off of mine.

He was a big guy, and it took all of my energy to get my body from underneath his.

My purse was still around my body, and I struggled to get to my phone. With shaky hands, I used my fingerprint to unlock it and held it down for Siri and requested 911.

When the operator answered, I said as loud as I could, "Help me."

KAMDEN

I didn't think my night could get any worse. Not only was my car fucked up, but the cops ended up cuffing me and shoving me in the back of the police car. Several more officers showed up, and it was a whole fuckin' mess. I had no idea what Vida told them, but I knew it wasn't the truth. I had no doubt that I was going to jail tonight.

One of the officers slid into the driver's seat and looked at me in the rearview mirror. He looked like an asshole, so I wasn't expecting him to be helpful.

"The young lady said you were assaulting her," he said.

I knew enough not to say shit. I just looked at him like he was crazy.

"There were a couple of witnesses that said they saw her breaking your windows with the crowbar we found next to your car."

I still didn't say shit. I was too angry, and there was no telling what would come out of my mouth. Too many Black men and women were being killed for doing absolutely nothing, and I didn't want to do anything to rub this asshole the wrong way. *Not that it would matter!*

"You're not gonna speak up on your own behalf?"

"Are you arresting me?"

"We haven't decided yet. We're trying to get to the bottom of the situation. If you could just answer a few questions—"

"Naw, I'm not answering no questions."

He gave me a frustrated look and got out. I wasn't about to answer shit without a lawyer present, so I didn't give one fuck if he was frustrated. Shit, I was frustrated, too. It was my truck that was fucked up and my ass sitting in the back of a police car in cuffs. *Yeah, that makes sense.*

About thirty minutes later, another officer opened the back door and roughly pulled me out. I stumbled to my feet, and he uncuffed me.

"You're free to go. If you'd like to press charges against the young lady, feel free to do so," he said.

I almost asked what happened that made them change their tune but thought, *fuck it!* I went back to my truck and got all my important information out, then pulled out my phone to call a tow truck. When I looked at the screen, I had multiple missed calls from damn near everybody in my family... except Jae. *Shit!*

I selected the contact for the last person that called me, which was Ms. Lynn.

"Kamden, Jae's in the ER. Someone attacked her in front of her house," she cried as soon as she answered.

I couldn't reply right away because I was trying to process her words. *Jae was attacked?*

"Hello! Kam, are you there?"

"I'm here, I—who would—is she okay?"

"I haven't seen her or a doctor yet. She was able to call 911, so I'm hoping that's a good sign. You need to get here."

"I'll be on the next flight."

Ending the call, I was at a loss for a minute. I finally got my girl, and someone tried to take her away from me. The thought filled me with sadness and anger at the same time. *Who would do this? Was it random or personal?*

"Aye, man. You good?" Vic said.

"No, I'm not. Jae was attacked in front of her house. She's been taken to the ER. I need to get on the next flight to Seattle, but I—"

"I gotchu, bruh. Kolby knew we were meeting this evening, and he called me when he couldn't reach you. He didn't tell me what happened, but it sounded urgent. I told him what was going down here, and he's on his way. I'm willing to bet he already booked a flight. I'll call a tow truck and send you the info. Let's go inside."

I didn't respond to Vic, but I heard him. By the time we got to the building, Kolby was pulling up.

"Thanks, Vic. I appreciate you looking out."

"Not a problem. I'll text you the info about your truck."

We gave each other some dap, and I hopped in Kolby's truck, then noticed Kyree was in the back. I put my belongings on the floor and closed the door. We rode to the airport in silence. When Kolby drove to the parking garage, it was then that I realized that he wasn't just dropping me off, but they were coming with me. I'd never been more grateful for my brothers than I was in that moment.

We didn't speak until we'd gone through security and made it to our gate. There was still an hour before they would start boarding the plane.

"You talked to Ms. Lynn?" Kolby asked.

My phone vibrated just as I was about to answer him. "This is her. Hello?"

"Hey, Kam. The doctor said that she has some bumps and bruises, but she's okay. I haven't seen her yet, but I will once they get her in a room."

"I'm at the airport, so I'll be there as soon as I can."

I ended the call and let out a deep sigh before relaying the information to my brothers. As I finished, another phone call came in from Myles.

"Wassup?"

"Once you check on Jae, come see me."

"Gotchu. My brothers will be with me."

"Cool."

"Who was that?" Kyree asked.

"Myles. He wants me to get with him after I see Jae."

"You think he knows something?" Kolby asked.

"I hope so."

FIVE HOURS LATER, we were headed to UW Medical Center ER. Seattle was two hours behind Chicago, so it was just after midnight. The ride was quiet. Actually, there hadn't been much talking since they picked me up. I was boiling inside and doing my best to keep my cool.

When we pulled into the parking lot of the hospital, I sent Ms. Lynn a text to find out what room Jae was in. She replied with the room number and said to enter through the ER.

We did as she instructed and were stopped by security. I didn't have the patience to deal with another person in that capacity, so I was thankful that my brothers were there to handle it. Thankfully, Kyree did all the talking, and Ms. Lynn had given him my name. He explained to us that because of the nature of the incident, they had to be careful. As he escorted us to Jae's room, he let us know that there was a police officer outside her room, as well, for extra precaution. I definitely appreciated their efforts to keep her safe.

When the door opened, Ms. Lynn turned around and immediately came to me with outstretched arms. While I hugged her, my eyes went to Jaelynn. I could see the bruising on her face from where I was standing. I released Ms. Lynn and went to Jae's side.

"Shit, baby girl."

Her delicate face was bruised and swollen on each side, and her lip was busted and swollen as well. My anger was close to boiling over in the form of tears. I swallowed the lump in my throat and leaned down to softly kiss her forehead, her nose, then her swollen lips before covering her hands with one of mine.

"Has she been awake?" I asked Ms. Lynn.

"She has, but... they had to sedate her when..." She approached me and took my free hand. "I'm so sorry, son. She lost the baby."

I felt like someone had ripped my heart out of my chest and gut punched me. My knees buckled, but my brothers were there to keep me on my feet. Ms. Lynn moved a chair over so that I could sit down. The tears that I was trying hard to keep at bay fell fast and furiously. My head went to my hands, and I silently cried for the loss of my child while my brothers and Ms. Lynn consoled me.

I had a feeling she was pregnant, but to have it confirmed, then taken away in the same moment... I couldn't begin to explain the level of pain I felt.

"The doctor already performed a D&C to—"

I shook my head because I didn't want to hear how the doctor scraped away the remains of my baby.

"Kam," I heard Jaelynn softly whisper.

I wiped my face quickly and stood, carefully hovering over her and getting as close to her as I could without hurting her. She was attempting to open her eyes, and I could see that they were swollen. Seeing her like that was really fucking with me, but I wanted to be strong for her. However, my emotions got the best of me, and it was impossible for me to hide them.

"Baby girl, I'm here."

"Kam, we—we—the baby—"

"Shh. I know, Jae. Don't worry about that right now."

"I'm sorry—"

"Naw, baby. This ain't your fault. Okay?"

I gently kissed her swollen lips, and our tears mixed together. I had no idea what to say to stop her tears, because I couldn't control my own. I pulled the chair closer to her bed, then sat down, still holding her hand.

"I love you so much, Jae. I'm just glad you're okay."

She slowly nodded as tears ran down her face. I kissed her hand, letting my lips linger there for a moment. My own face was still wet with tears that wouldn't stop falling.

"Whatever I need to do to help you get through this, I'll do it, Jae. You're my whole world, baby girl. I—"

"It was Drew, Kam! I shot him! I shot Drew! Is he dead?" She was becoming hysterical, and I had no idea what she was talking about.

"Shh. Calm down."

"Is he dead? Did I kill him? I had to shoot him. He was gonna—"

"Go get the nurse!" Ms. Lynn shouted to anybody.

"Please, Jae. Calm down. It's okay."

The nurse rushed in as Jaelynn had another outburst.

"He made me lose the baby," she cried. "He slammed me and kicked me. Kam, I lost the baby. I'm sorry. I—"

"It's okay. We'll be okay."

"What if he's not dead? What if he comes after me? Kam—"

"Shhh, baby girl. Shhh."

I sat on the edge of the bed and gently wrapped my arms around her, consoling her as best I could. The nurse put something in her IV, and almost immediately, she calmed down. I held her in my arms until I felt her body relax, then gently laid her back on the pillow.

"She should be out for a while. Let me know if you need anything else."

"Ms. Lynn, what happened?"

"I didn't know any of the details until a little while ago, and they're still choppy," Ms. Lynn explained. "A man attacked her in front of her house. She was able to get to her gun, and she shot him. When the police officers came to talk to Jae, she was out cold.

They told me she shot her attacker three times, and he was in surgery—"

"They're trying to save the muthafucka after he—"

"Kam, calm down," Kyree said.

"Fuck you mean? That nigga attacked her, and—"

"Chill, bruh." Kyree tried again.

I took a deep breath and looked over at Jaelynn. She looked to be sleeping peacefully.

"Excuse my language, Ms. Lynn. I'm just—"

"No need to apologize, son. I feel the same way you do."

"Ms. Lynn, I want to talk to my brothers real quick in the hallway. When I'm done, you can head home and get some rest."

"Are you sure?"

"Positive. I'll be right back."

We quietly left the room and walked down the hallway so that the officer on guard didn't hear our conversation.

"You good, bruh? A lot of shit went down tonight," Kolby asked.

"I'm more worried about Jae than I am myself. I have to be strong for her, no matter how I feel. She's been through so much already. Now we lost our—" I felt myself getting choked up and couldn't finish.

"Taking care of Jae is important, but you can't do that if you ain't okay. We're here for whatever you need, bruh," Kyree said with a hand on my shoulder.

"I know. I appreciate y'all riding out with me. I didn't know what I was walking into. Can y'all go see what's up with Myles and let him know I couldn't leave Jae? Tell him a nigga named Drew attacked her. I have no idea who the fuck that is."

"You think it's another ex?" Kolby asked.

"Naw, I don't think so."

"We'll talk to Myles. He probably knows more than the cops at this point," Kolby said.

We hugged, and I told them I'd send Ms. Lynn out so she could leave with them. When I entered Jae's room, Ms. Lynn was standing next to Jae's bed, looking down at her.

"I didn't know she had a gun, but I'm glad she did," Ms. Lynn spoke softly with her back to me.

"Yeah, she actually mentioned it to me that last time I was here. I'm glad she wasn't afraid to use it to protect herself. This could have turned out a lot differently."

She leaned down and kissed a sleeping Jaelynn's cheek, then turned around to give me a hug.

"My brothers are waiting in the hallway to walk out with you. Get some rest, and I'll take care of her. I'll see you in the morning."

She nodded and left Jaelynn and me alone. I sat next to her in the chair and rested my head on the bed next to her leg. I wanted to hear from Jaelynn what happened, but I knew it might be a while before she was able to talk about it without becoming hysterical.

I closed my eyes and thanked God for sparing her life, even if He didn't spare the life of our unborn child. Thinking about how much time we wasted over the last year and a half made me wish I would have tried harder to make her mine instead of allowing her to control the narrative. Now that I had her, there was nothing I wouldn't do for her.

JAELYNN

When I opened my eyes, the room was dark, but there was light coming through the slits in the blinds. I tried to turn my head to the right, but my neck was very stiff. I lifted my hand and felt around on the bed. When I felt what I knew was Kamden's head, I felt relieved.

"Babe," I whispered, while rubbing his cheek.

When he lifted his head and his eyes landed on me, he gave me a smile, but I could see exhaustion all over his face.

"Hey, baby girl. You good?"

"I'm in pain physically, mentally, and emotionally, but you're here, so I'll be okay."

"I'm gonna go get the nurse to give you some pain meds."

"No, not yet. They make me sleepy. Did I kill him?"

"Jae, who is this nigga?"

"Drew is Drake's brother. He—umm—he was going to—to rape me. I swear I hope he died. He took our baby away. He doesn't deserve to live."

I could feel myself getting worked up. "Calm down, baby girl, please," Kamden pleaded. "I don't want you worrying about shit but getting better. I haven't heard anything about Drew. If you didn't kill him, somebody will."

"You think the nurse or doctor will tell me?"

"Jae, that's not a priority right now. You hungry?" he asked.

If my eyes weren't swollen, I'd roll them. "I don't have an appetite, but I probably should eat."

"Your mom went home to get some sleep and take a shower. I'll have her bring you some soup because I'm sure you don't want whatever they're serving."

Before I could answer, a nurse walked in. Kamden moved away from the bed and took out his phone.

"Good morning, Ms. Waters. I'm Nurse Taylor. How are you feeling?"

I couldn't see her face because she was holding two bouquets of flowers.

"Good morning. Very sore. Can you give me the cards that came with the flowers?"

She gave me the cards, and I thanked her. "There are several bouquets for you at the nurse's station. I could only handle a couple."

"Really? Wow! I wonder who they're from?"

I opened one of the cards, and all it read was *Get Well Soon*. The second card read, *Best Wishes*.

"Do you want me to bring them all in? It's gonna fill your room," she asked.

"Can you bring a couple more in and just the cards to the rest of them? If possible, you can give the flowers to some other patients."

"That's very nice of you. Flowers will definitely brighten someone's day. I'm so sorry this happened to you, sweetheart. Unfortunately, you're going to be sore for a week or two. Are you hungry?" She opened the blinds while she spoke.

"I'm not, but I'm gonna eat. My mom is gonna bring me some soup. Can I ask you a question?"

"Sure."

"Do you know if the person who attacked me is alive?"

"Oh, I'm not sure, sweetheart. I wasn't here when you were brought in. Your file only tells me about why you're here. Maybe Dr. Seagram will be able to tell you when she comes in."

"Okay. Thanks." She looked like she was telling the truth so I wouldn't press her.

"I'm gonna take your vitals and remove the IV and the catheter. Then we'll get you moving and cleaned up."

While the nurse did what she needed to do, I reflected on the events of the last several hours. I couldn't believe that Drew tried to rape me. *Who raised these niggas?* When Drake and I dated, Drew was always disrespectful toward me, causing Drake to have to defend me often. I never understood his beef with me. I assumed he simply didn't like me. It seems like what came off as him not liking me was actually him being pissed that I chose Drake instead of him. The look in his eyes was that of pure hatred. I hoped his bitch ass suffered the same fate as his brother.

When I found out that I'd lost the baby, I completely lost it, and they had to sedate me. Nothing I'd experienced in my life had ever caused me to feel pain so deeply than when I heard those words. I lost a part of me that could never be replaced, and I knew it was gonna be a battle getting over it, if ever. If Drew was dead, he got what he deserved. I wasn't an evil person at all, but I hoped he suffered ten times the pain he caused me.

"Okay, let's get you up," said Nurse Taylor, pulling me out of my thoughts.

"I got her," Kamden offered.

He came over to the side of the bed to help me up. It pained me to sit all the way up, but I pushed through. After taking a few deep breaths, I moved my legs over the edge of the bed.

"You ready?" Kamden asked.

"Yeah."

He bent down low enough for me to put one of my arms

around his shoulders. Pushing off the bed with my free hand, my feet touched the floor, and I was standing with the help of Kamden. Once I was stable, I moved the arm that was on his shoulders to his waist.

"One step at a time, Jae."

It seemed like it took forever to move the three or four feet to the bathroom, but I eventually made it. As I adjusted my body to sit on the toilet, I caught a glimpse of my face and was startled. I almost didn't recognize myself.

"Shit," I whispered.

When Kamden noticed that I was looking in the mirror, he stood in front of me to block my view.

"Those bruises will heal, Jae."

"I know, but—"

"Shh. No more mirrors until you heal. I don't want you worrying about how you look."

He took the hand towel that was on the rack and put it over the mirror.

"Do you want me to stay in here while you use the bathroom?" Kamden asked.

"No, but can you help me take a shower?"

"Anything you need, Jae. I'll be right back. Don't look in that mirror."

He started the shower, then left me alone to relieve my bladder. It took a while for the stream of liquid to begin to flow. When it did, it was like I'd drank a gallon of water. A wave of sadness washed over me when I wiped myself and saw blood on the toilet paper. Instead of dwelling on it, I flushed the toilet and used the wall to help me stand.

The bathroom door opened, and Kamden stepped inside, locking it behind him. He put the towels he was holding on the sink, then began to undress, causing me to look at him in confusion.

"What are you doing?" I asked.

"About to help you shower?"

"Do you have a change of clothes?"

"Ms. Lynn is gonna grab me something from your house."

I'd forgotten that he'd claimed my extra bedroom as his when we were just friends. He'd always leave a few things there when he visited. I guess that was convenient for a time such as this.

Once he was naked, he picked up the two small towels and stepped into the shower, then held his hand out to help me. When we were both inside, he gently wrapped his arms around me as we stood under the stream of water.

I rested my head on his chest and snaked my arms through his to hold him around his waist. I allowed myself to relax for the first time since I was attacked. Being in Kamden's arms didn't change anything that happened, but having him there made dealing with it easier.

"I wanna try again," I said.

He kissed the top of my head. "Whenever you're ready."

"As soon as the doctor says we can."

He pulled away from me, and I looked up at him. "Whenever you're ready," he repeated.

Grabbing the tiny bar of hospital-issued soap, he lathered up one of the towels before using it to bathe me. He was so gentle; I could barely feel the towel as it grazed my body.

"Tell me if I'm hurting you."

He kneeled down to wash my bottom half, and I felt his lips brush against my stomach before he rested his head there, then put his arms around my waist. My hands went to his head, and I felt his chest heave against my legs. I comforted him as best I could, while his tears flowed down the drain.

A few minutes later, as if nothing happened, he released me and went back to washing me up. When he got back to his feet, he tried to avoid my eyes. I grabbed his chin and made him face me.

"Babe, you don't have to be strong in front of me. I know you're hurting, too."

"I keep thinking that if I had made you stay with me a few more days or adjusted my schedule and left with you, our baby would still be growing inside of you."

"Kam, there is only one person to blame for this, and it's not either of us. I've gone over in my head what I could have done differently as well, but we aren't to blame, babe."

"I love you."

"I love you, too."

He leaned down and kissed my lips, then turned me around so I could rinse off. While I did that, he bathed himself. He turned the water off after he'd rinsed himself.

"Your sisters are going crazy. You need to call them soon," he told me.

He finished drying me off and made sure the towel was wrapped around me securely. I waited for him to dry himself off and wrap the towel around his waist. When we walked out of the bathroom, Nurse Taylor turned around. Her eyes went straight to Kamden.

"Umm, can you excuse us for a minute?" I asked.

She was so focused on him that she didn't reply.

"Nurse Taylor!" I said a little louder. "Can you leave, please?"

"Oh, umm, yes. I'll come back shortly, when you're, umm, dressed."

She still didn't take her eyes off Kamden. I couldn't even be mad at her, though. He was fine as hell and she could probably see his dick print through the towel.

"Dang, Kam. You got that middle-aged white lady checking you out." I teased when she was gone.

"That lady better go sit her ass in the corner somewhere. If I was even remotely interested, she wouldn't know what to do with all this dick." He groped himself to add emphasis before helping me put the gown on that Nurse Taylor had left on the bed.

I noticed she had changed the linen, as well.

"What the hell is this?" Kamden asked as he held up a pair of hospital-issued mesh underwear, along with a pad.

I took them from him, rolling my eyes. "These are panties, and this is a pad. Now help me put them on."

He helped me put the underwear on, and I secured the pad in the crotch before pulling them all the way up.

"I should have asked your mom to bring some of your toiletries. That cheap ass soap and this watered down lotion gon' have our skin dry as hell."

"I'll be fine."

Once he rubbed me down with lotion, he helped me get back in bed and tucked me in. My mom entered the room with bags in hand. She and Kamden greeted each other, and she gave him the bag with his clothes before he went back to the bathroom to get dressed.

"Hey, sweetheart. How you feeling?" Ma asked.

"Still sore, Ma, but I'm okay."

"I had some soup at home, and I was able to doctor it up for you. You ready to eat now?"

Before I could answer, Nurse Taylor walked back in just as Kamden came out of the bathroom. I watched her as she ogled my man. When Kamden caught her looking, she looked away. I giggled inside at the whole thing.

"Baby girl, I'm gonna step out real quick and call my brothers."

As he was leaving, Dr. Seagram came in. I vaguely remembered seeing her yesterday.

"Good morning, Ms. Waters. I'm Dr. Seagram. We met yesterday, but I know everything is kind of a blur. How are you feeling today?"

"My body is still pretty sore."

"That's to be expected. How about here and here?" She pointed to her head and her heart.

I was a bit surprised by her question and couldn't give her an answer, so she continued.

"What you've been through would break even the strongest person. I need you to know that whatever you're feeling is okay, no matter what it is. Sadness, anger, fear, frustration, despair... whatever it is. You have a right to feel it all."

I nodded as tears welled up in my eyes. I felt my mom's hand rubbing my leg in a comforting manner.

"Here are some pamphlets that have some information that might be helpful. I strongly recommend therapy, for you and your fiancé."

"Thank you. I appreciate it. Can I ask you a question?"

She nodded as I took the pamphlets from her hand.

"Do you know what happened to the guy that attacked me? I know I shot him three times. Is he still alive?"

"I'm sorry, I don't," was all she said.

I had a feeling she knew something but didn't want to say. "Oh, okay. Thank you. When will I be able to go home?"

"Honestly, there's no *medical* reason that you can't be released today. However, it would do my heart good if you'd stay one more night. Just for my own peace of mind."

"Okay. I'll stay for another night. Thank you again for your care and concern. It means a lot."

"You're welcome."

She grabbed my chart from Nurse Taylor and looked it over. After asking me several questions, she did her own assessment of my physical condition and promised to check on me before her shift ended. Once she and Nurse Taylor were gone, my mom prepared my soup.

"It's still pretty hot." She informed me, handing me a thermos lid full of soup and a spoon.

"Thanks, Ma."

"When you finish, you need to call your sisters. They are in full panic mode, even though everyone has told them that you're fine."

"Can you just call them now and put them on speaker? Not on FaceTime. I don't want them to see my face."

My mom busied herself with her phone and connected a call with Braelynn.

"Hold on Brae. Let me get My on the phone."

There was a short silence before Myla picked up, and my mom merged the calls.

"I'm with Jae," Ma said.

Both of them started talking at the same time.

"Can't nobody understand y'all talking at the same time. Brae, you go first."

"Sis, we have a lot of questions, but we really just wanted to hear your voice and know you're good?"

"I'm okay."

"I know there's nothing we can say or do to make you feel better, but we're praying for you and Kam," Myla said.

"We wanted to come, but our husbands thought it would be better if they went instead."

"I know y'all want to be here, but the guys were right. Kam is taking good care of me, and his brothers are making sure he's good."

"Okay. We love you!"

"Love you more."

"Bye, Ma," Braelynn said before the call ended.

"Glad to see you're eating, baby girl," Kamden said when he reentered the room.

"It's good. You want some?"

"Naw, I'm good. So what did the doctor say?"

"She gave me some pamphlets, suggested counseling, and said I could go home today, but she'd prefer if I stayed another day."

He nodded. "Are you staying?"

"Yeah."

"Okay. Umm, there are some officers here to see you. Do you feel up to talking to them?"

"It's fine."

He kissed me before going to get the officers. I had to take a deep breath and get my mind right for the conversation that was about to take place.

KAMDEN

I couldn't think of a time in my life when I'd been more exhausted, mentally, and physically. If I could, I'd hop on a plane and take Jaelynn to an island for three months. Somewhere with no phones, no internet, no television—just me and her with no interruptions or distractions. Since that wasn't possible, I needed to do whatever I could to help her get through this traumatic experience.

When I spoke to my brothers, they informed me that they'd be picking me up in about an hour. They'd been at Myles's house since the wee hours. We didn't want to talk about the situation on the phone, so I was still in the dark about what Myles may have told them. As I was finishing up my call with them, I called two of my supervisors to let them know what was going on. I gave them some instructions for the next couple of days and told them I'd be checking in. When I ended that call, two police officers approached Jaelynn's room. They spoke to the officer that was guarding her room, and then their eyes landed on me.

"How can I help you, Officers?"

"We're here to speak with Jaelynn Waters. You are?"

"Her fiancé, Kamden Ross. Let me make sure she's decent."

I entered her room and saw that she was eating the soup that Ms. Lynn had brought her.

"Glad to see you're eating," I said.

"It's good. You want some?"

"Naw, I'm good. So what did the doctor say?"

"She gave me some pamphlets, suggested counseling, and said I could go home today, but she'd prefer if I stayed another day."

"Are you staying?"

"Yeah."

"Okay. Umm, there are some officers here to see you. Do you feel up to talking to them?"

"It's fine."

I kissed her before going to get the officers. Opening the door, I waved them in, then sat on the edge of Jaelynn's bed between her and the officers. Ms. Lynn was on the other side.

"Hi, Ms. Waters. I'm Officer Jenkins, and this is my partner, Officer Nethers. We wanted to ask you a few questions about the attack."

"Before I say anything, I need to know if my life is in danger. Will he come after me again?"

That was smart. She didn't come right out and ask if he was dead.

"Ma'am, your attacker didn't survive. Two of the bullets hit him in his chest, although they missed the vital organs, he lost too much blood and didn't survive the surgery."

Lucky muthafucka!

Jaelynn couldn't hide the look of relief. "Okay," she replied.

"Can you walk us through what happened?" Jenkins asked.

"I pulled into my driveway and gathered my things before getting out of the car. I got my gun out of the glove compartment and put it in my purse, which was strapped around my body. I was holding a bag of food and a Walgreen's bag in my left hand. When I got out, I went to get my suitcase from the trunk. As I walked toward my house, I heard someone call my name. Before I could react, he grabbed the hood of my coat and said, 'I never could stand your bougie ass! You picked the wrong brother.'"

She paused and took a deep breath. I hated that she had to relive this shit.

Nethers spoke for the first time. "What do you think he meant?"

"I used to date his brother, Drake, but we broke up over two years ago. The first time I met them, they both were trying to get my number, but I ending up giving it to Drake."

"As in Drake Michaels?"

She nodded.

"Drake was found—"

"I heard about what happened to Drake."

"May I ask why you broke up?" came from Jenkins.

"Is that really relevant?" I intervened.

"Well—"

"It's not. You don't have to answer that, Jae."

Jenkins gave me a dirty look, but I didn't give a damn. Why her and Drake broke up had nothing to do with this situation.

"Do you think Drew was still upset that you decided to date Drake instead of him?" asked Jenkins.

"I guess so. When Drake and I were dating, Drew didn't seem to be very fond of me. He was always very rude and disrespectful. My relationship with Drake caused a big rift between them."

"Interesting," Nethers commented.

"They lived together, and because of Drew, we didn't spend much time at their place."

Both officers were jotting things down on little notepads, then Jenkins said, "Back to the night of the attack."

Jaelynn continued to recount the incident. This was my first time hearing everything that happened, and it was hard for me to listen. As a real man, knowing that your woman went through something so terrible and you weren't there to protect her, was a hard pill to swallow. However, knowing Jaelynn was brave enough to protect herself filled me with pride. I was glad she killed that nigga.

"One last thing. Do you always carry your gun with you, or—" Jenkins began before I interrupted.

"Why does that matter? She's licensed to carry. I'm sure y'all checked all that already."

He took a deep breath and didn't try to hide his irritation with me. *Nigga, fuck you!*

"Based on what you've said, your injuries, the attacker's injuries, and what we saw at the scene, your story checks out."

I couldn't help but frown up my face at this nigga.

"If we have any further questions, is there a number at which we can contact you?" Nethers spoke again.

"You can contact me, and I'll make sure you connect," I said.

This time, I got a dirty look from both officers, but they could definitely go somewhere and eat a dick. I gave no fucks about them having an attitude. After writing down my number, they left.

"You okay?"

"Honestly, I am. Now that I know he's dead, I feel better. I know that's bad to say, but it's the truth."

"Sweetheart, that man tried to rape you, and he may have killed you if you hadn't been prepared to protect yourself. I'm glad you're the one that's still breathing instead of him," Ms. Lynn told her.

"I feel the same way, Jae. It was either you or him. You did what you had to do."

"Jae, how long have you had a gun?" her mom asked.

"Umm, a couple of years."

"Really? What made you get one? Did you take a class to learn how to use it?"

Ms. Lynn really seemed intrigued, but I knew Jaelynn wasn't gonna tell her the real reason she became a gun owner.

"I was a single woman, living alone. I figured it was a good idea.

They have places you can go, and they teach you everything you need to know, including how to shoot."

"I'm so glad you were prepared. I don't know what I would have done if I'd lost you," Ms. Lynn said, leaning in to give her a gentle hug. "Maybe I should take that class."

"Me too, Ma. I never expected to actually shoot someone, but I'm glad I was ready. It wouldn't be a bad idea for you to be able to protect yourself."

"Jae, my brothers should—"

Before I finished my statement, there was a tap on the door. I summoned them in, and Myles, Kolby, and Kyree appeared.

"Hey, baby sis." Myles greeted, followed by my brothers.

I moved away from the bed so the three of them could give her a hug.

"You feel okay?" Kyree asked.

"Better I guess."

"Jae, since your mom is here, I'm gonna go grab a bite with them before their flight. Is that cool?"

"I'll be here when you get back." She joked.

"You better be." I kissed her lips a few times. "I love you."

"I love you, too."

When we left, nobody said a word until we got in the car, and Myles was the first to speak.

"So Jae killed that nigga, huh?"

"The cops left right before y'all came. They said she shot his ass three times, two were in the chest. He lost too much blood and didn't survive the surgery."

"If he had lived, he was gon' die. It was just a matter of when and how." Myles assured.

"I told her the same thing."

"How is she feeling about everything? Shit, how are you feeling?"

That was Kyree. He'd always been the more sensitive Ross brother, constantly checking on everybody.

"She will definitely be increasing her therapy sessions, and I'll probably join her for a few. Considering all that's happened, she's a lot tougher than I would have guessed."

"Jae is a 'G', no doubt." Myles added. "I know you're probably worried about them connecting the dots."

"Should I be?"

I'd thought about the possibility of the authorities connecting me to Drake's murder, but from what Myles had told me, it would be impossible.

"Naw, not at all, bruh. Just wanted to see where your head was at. It's all taken care of."

Myles was a mysterious muthafucka. I was glad we were on his good side. I'd learned not to ask him too many questions, and it looked like my brothers knew that as well. He'd tell you what he wanted you to know when he wanted you to know it, and that was that.

We found a spot to grab a quick bite before heading to the airport. After dropping Kyree and Kolby off, I took Myles home and drove the rental car back to the hospital, where I planned to be until Jaelynn was released the following day.

JAELYNN

*A*fter being released from the hospital, I was shocked and happy when we arrived at my house to find Braelynn and Myla there. However, when they saw my face, we all ended up in tears.

"Man, Jae, I can't believe this shit," Braelynn cried. "That punk ass nigga really tried it. I'm so glad you blasted his ass."

"When did you even get a gun?" Myla asked as she wiped her tears.

"After that shit with Drake. What are y'all doing here?"

"We listened to our husbands when all this shit happened, but we couldn't hold off seeing you any longer."

Apparently, as soon as their husbands landed, they hopped on the next flight. I swear I loved my girls. I prayed everyone had a Braelynn and Myla in their lives because they were truly a blessing.

"How are you, sis? What do you need us to do? Are you hungry?" Braelynn quizzed.

"Brae, chill," I told her as I sat on the edge of my bed.

As much as I loved that my girls were here, Braelynn was doing too much.

"Brae, give her some time. She's only been home thirty minutes." Myla cosigned.

Braelynn had the nerve to pout. It hadn't been too long since the last time I'd seen her, but her stomach looked like it was poking out a little more. Of course I was happy for her, but seeing her reminded me that my baby was gone, and it saddened me.

"Okay, fine. We got plenty to do anyway." She resigned.

"Which is what?" I asked.

"Kamden has put us in charge of packing up all your shit. He's not leaving here without you." Myla informed me.

Well, damn!

"Oh okay." I started to stand, and the two of them looked at me like I was crazy.

"What are you doing?" Braelynn asked.

"About to help y'all pack."

"Jae, if you don't sit your ass down somewhere," Kamden said, startling me when he walked in the room.

"Seriously, Jae. We got this." Myla assured. "We'll start in one of the other rooms."

"Do y'all have boxes?"

"A few. Ma and Uncle David are bringing over more," Braelynn replied. They left, closing the door behind them, as Kamden sat next to me.

"You heard Dr. Seagram tell you to take it easy. You need to chill and let us handle everything. The plan is to have everything you want to take packed by the end of the week. You just need to let me know what you're leaving and find someone we can give or donate it to."

"Okay."

"Your phone is charging in the kitchen. Danae and Tori have texted you several times, checking on you. Dr. Femi called a few times, too. I checked your Facebook and Instagram, and it looks like people heard the story on the news or online. You got a ton of messages from people, wishing you well."

"That's nice to know," I said before covering my mouth as I yawned.

"Yeah. Everybody ain't evil. You tired?"

"I am. Can we shower and take a nap?"

I knew that he hadn't had much sleep the past two nights while I was in the hospital. He slept in a chair that he pulled up right next to the bed both nights, even though they offered to bring him a cot. At one point, I begged him to get in the bed with me, and he did, for a while. But the nurses kept coming in doing what nurses did, so that didn't last long.

"Of course, baby girl."

About twenty minutes later, we were showered. After he gently rubbed me down with some of my body butter, I put on one of his T-shirts and a pair of boy shorts. Unfortunately, I still had some light bleeding, which meant I had to wear a pad. I didn't use them normally because my period was usually very light. All I had were the ones from the hospital, and they felt like diapers. Kamden put on a pair of basketball shorts, and just as we were about to settle into bed, there was a knock on the door.

"Come in," Kamden said.

"Mrs. Atwood just dropped this off. She said it was left out front after the incident, and she didn't want anyone rummaging through your things."

Braelynn rolled in my suitcase and the bag from Walgreens. She turned around and left just as fast as she came, closing the door on her way out. Kamden took the Walgreens bag from around the suitcase handle and rolled the suitcase to the corner. He joined me in bed, where I was sitting up under the comforter and gave me the bag.

I absently looked through it, seeing all the items that I'd purchased that night, and when my eyes landed on the pregnancy test, my heart sank. I threw the bag across the room and screamed at the top of my lungs.

"Whhhhyyyyyy! Bad things keep happening to me, Kam!"

His arms were around me in a flash, and my bedroom door swung open. Braelynn and Myla stood there with worried expressions, and Kamden waved them away. They were reluctant to leave, but they did.

"Shh, baby girl. I know it hurts. Let it out." He rubbed my back as he spoke comforting words.

"I'm a good person. What did I do to—"

"Jae, you're perfect. Bad things happen to good people all the time. I don't know why."

"It hurts so much. I didn't even get to take a test or be excited about our baby."

"I know. I'm hurt too, but we gon' get through this shit, okay. Our baby can't be replaced, but you gon' have so many of my babies that you won't know what to do. I promise you."

His words were consoling, but I found myself wishing that I could go to sleep and wake up a year from now, holding our baby in my arms. While I cried, he leaned against the headboard and I rested my head on his lap. We remained in that position until I eventually dozed off.

HOURS LATER, I woke up to darkness, snug in Kamden's arms. When I tried to move, he unconsciously held me in place. I still had some swelling in my face, and my body was still sore. At the moment, though, all that mattered was being in his arms, so I remained resting on his chest with one of his arms around my shoulders, cradling me.

My mind flashed back to the slight breakdown I had before I fell asleep. I knew that the healing process wouldn't be easy and more breakdowns were likely to occur. I had to remember that this too shall pass and to take it one day... one hour... hell, one minute at a time.

When I could no longer hold my bladder, I tapped Kamden on the chest to wake him up.

"Wassup, baby girl?"

"I need to use the bathroom."

"You need help?"

"No, I need you to let me up."

"Oh shit. My bad."

He released me from his hold, and I slowly eased out of bed and went to relieve my bladder. When I came back, he had turned on the lamp and was sitting up with his back against the headboard. I got back in bed, and he motioned for me to sit on his lap, and I did, adjusting my legs so that they extended to the side.

"I love you so much, Jae."

I put my arms around his neck, and our lips connected in a tender kiss. We enjoyed the simple touching of our lips, with no tongue, for an extended amount of time. He pulled away but continued pecking my lips, my cheeks, the tip of my nose, and finally, my forehead.

"I love you, too."

"Remember the first time we were in Belize? We went to that club, and y'all were shaking y'all asses for all the niggas in the club."

"We were not."

"Hell yeah you were. Right before we came to snatch y'all off the floor, I told Kyree I was good on you 'cause you'd have my ass in jail."

"First of all, you didn't snatch me off the floor. You tried it, but I had to shut that shit down."

"I know, and you proved my point. Had my ass arguing with you in the middle of the dance floor about why you couldn't be doing all that extra shit. I wanted to snatch you up so bad. But I knew you would resist and I wasn't trying to go to jail in Belize."

"You weren't the boss of me."

"You made that perfectly clear. I was surprised you were cool with staying in the room with me."

"Truthfully, I wanted to strangle Myla when she asked me, but I didn't want to be a party pooper. Plus, I was trying to prove to myself that I wasn't attracted to you. You weren't thinking about me anyway."

"Shit! Yes the hell I was."

"Kam, there were a few nights that you stayed out all night."

"Jae, the nights I stayed in the room with you, my dick was hard all fuckin' night. I ain't gon' lie; a few of those nights, I had to go find me a couple of shorties to bust a quick nut. Whole time, I had you on my mind. I think I even called one of them by your name."

"Wow, Kam. That's trifling."

"A nigga had to do what he had to do." He kissed me again. "But it was all worth it, right?"

I nodded.

We sat quietly for a moment, enjoying each other's presence. I could tell that Kamden was thinking hard about something because he was biting the corner of his lip.

Finally, he asked, "Do you mind if I sit in on some of your therapy sessions?"

"Why would I mind? I think I have one scheduled for tomorrow or the day after. You should come."

"I will. Every time I think about what we lost, I wanna bring that nigga back to life and kill him myself."

"I know, babe. I know."

KAMDEN

*T*he next two weeks were slightly overwhelming. Braelynn and Myla went back to Chicago after a couple of days. They got a good amount of packing done, and I think having them there brightened Jaelynn's spirits. When they left, we still had a lot of packing to do. Ms. Lynn, Ms. Delilah, Myles, and Uncle David were a great help. One or more of them was there every day to help out, and we were grateful.

Unfortunately, Jaelynn had been having nightmares, and it was really fucking with me. I hated that I couldn't do anything to make them go away. Dr. Femi was able to see her several times, and I'd gone with her at least half of those times. I'd never felt the need to seek therapy, but I was never opposed if it was necessary. I found it to be beneficial, and although Jaelynn was still having nightmares, therapy was helping her in other ways.

Talking to Dr. Femi helped me a lot because she helped me understand that my feelings were valid and that I had every right to feel them. I admitted that I was angry with God for not protecting our unborn child, and I felt guilty for having those feelings. It was crazy because she told me the same thing that I told Jaelynn. Bad things happened to good people all the time and nobody knew why. I believed that but hadn't applied it to myself.

After being in Seattle for fourteen days, we were finally back in Chicago. The process of moving someone halfway across the country wasn't something I ever wanted to do again. The furniture that she decided to keep would be brought to Chicago by the moving company we hired and put in storage, along with a lot of her clothing and some other things. Her car was being transported from Seattle and would be in Chicago in a couple of days.

Kyree and Braelynn picked us up from the airport, and we were headed to my parents' house for dinner. My mother hadn't seen Jaelynn since the day I proposed, and if we didn't come for dinner, I'd never hear the end of it.

"Have you talked to Vic about your car?" Kyree asked.

"Yeah, I lucked up."

"How so?"

"One of his cousins owns a tow truck company. Vic explained to him everything that was going on, and he charged for the tow but not for the storage. I'll figure that shit out tomorrow."

"What are y'all talking about? What the hell happened to your car?" Jaelynn asked.

So much happened since that night that I didn't realize that I hadn't told Jaelynn about Vida's crazy ass.

"Damn, I forgot to tell you. Remember I told you I had a meeting with Vic, the realtor?"

She nodded.

"The office is in a strip mall, and when I was walking in, I ran into Vida. We exchanged a few words, and I basically dismissed her because she was talking crazy. About ten minutes into my meeting, one of Vic's coworkers came in and told us to come outside. When I got out there, Vida had busted out all my windows and slashed all my tires."

"What? Babe, you can't be serious."

"As hell. She was still swinging when I got to my car. I had to snatch the crowbar away from her. I was so pissed. To make it worse, somebody called the cops, and I almost got arrested. They cuffed me and put me in the back of the police car while they figured what happened."

"Damn! How is it that she fucked up your car, yet you ended up in cuffs? That's crazy."

"When the cop let me out and uncuffed me, I didn't even bother asking him why. He told me I could press charges against Vida if I wanted to."

"Hell the fuck yeah you want to. If you let that hoe get away with that shit, me and you gon' have a problem."

Jaelynn probably only weighed a hundred and thirty pounds, soaking wet, but she stayed trying to boss up on somebody.

"What kinda problem me and you gon' have, baby girl?" I leaned over and kissed her cheek.

"A problem you don't want. We're going tomorrow."

"Whatever you say, Jae. I don't want no smoke from you." I chuckled, and she pushed me in the shoulder.

"But seriously, Kam, she might be *crazy*, crazy. If you don't press charges, she might do some more crazy shit." Braelynn added.

"I'd like to think she had a brief moment of insanity. She didn't seem crazy when we were dating."

"They never do," Kyree mumbled. He definitely had a crazy experience with the woman he was dating before Braelynn.

"Okay, I'm tired of talking about that hoe. You're pressing charges tomorrow," Jae said.

"Calm your little ass down. I already agreed with you."

We continued to converse on the ride to my parents' house. When we got there, Kolby and Myla's truck was parked on one side of my parents' driveway, and Kyree parked next to them. We got out and opened the doors for the girls, then headed inside.

As soon as my mother laid eyes on Jaelynn, she damn near bum-rushed her. I let them have their moment and walked further into the house. When my dad saw me, he nodded his head toward the back of the house, and I followed him.

"Wassup, Dad? Everything good?"

"That's what I want to ask you. We didn't talk much while you were in Seattle, and I wanted to make sure you were okay."

"Honestly, I'm taking it one day at a time. My priority is Jaelynn."

"As it should be, but sometimes, when things like this happen, men get lost in the shuffle. People tend to forget that we have feelings, too. I'm sure what happened to Jaelynn tore you apart, and losing your baby made it much worse."

"It's been hard, Dad. Really hard. But we've been going to therapy, and it's been helping."

"I'm proud of you, Kam. Some people, especially us Black folks, are too proud to admit when they need help. I'm glad that you aren't one of those people. Always remember that I'm here if you need to talk, anytime, day or night."

"Thanks, Dad. I appreciate you."

"I love you, son."

"I love you, too, Dad."

By the time we went back to the family room, everyone was there, and we were good and ready to eat. Jaelynn had a smile on her face, and when our eyes connected, I mouthed, *you good*, and she nodded.

After taking a few minutes to wash our hands, we all made our way to the dining room. I looked around as we all got situated and couldn't help but smile. It was crazy how just a couple of years ago, it was just me, my brothers, and my parents. Now, there were five more people here, and as small as the twins still were, they brought so much love, energy, and life to our family. Soon, Braelynn and Kyree would be adding their little bundle of joy to the mix, and hopefully, so would Jaelynn and I.

My dad blessed the food, and for a few minutes, casserole dishes were passed around the table as we filled our plates. My mom made fried chicken, mac and cheese, green beans, and sweet potatoes. I promise nobody said shit for a good five minutes, not even the babies, as they munched on their food.

"So Kamden..." Ma started.

I could tell by her tone that she was about to be on some bull.

"What do you plan to do about that old crazy girl that messed up your car?"

"Oh, Ms. Stella, we pressing charges tomorrow," Jaelynn answered before I had a chance.

"I tell you what, you boys better be lucky y'all picked the right ones to settle down with because y'all would have seen a different side of me had you not."

"You act like we've never seen your other side." Kyree instigated.

"You're the last one to be talking! That was nothing compared to what it would've been had y'all married and procreated with some crazy lil' heffa. Leah almost made me step outside myself, but thank God we dodged that bullet."

Leah, Kyree's crazy ex, tried to pin a baby on him that wasn't his. She had a whole other nigga almost the whole time they were dating.

"Why you gotta bring her up?" Kyree complained.

"Because you had to add your two cents. But back to the topic at hand, I'm glad you're pressing charges against her. That'll teach her behind a lesson."

"Dad, get your wife," I told him.

He shook his head. "She's right this time."

She frowned her nose up at him. "Excuse me! I'm always right. Don't play with me."

"You see what you did? That's why I keep my mouth shut around here. Don't be putting me in y'all mess," he fussed.

Everyone at the table laughed, and dinner proceeded with more of the same. It was always a good time when we got together. When we were done eating, the ladies cleaned up, and we took the twins to the family room. After a few hours, the twins started to get fussy, and everyone took that as the cue that it was time to go.

I was ready to go home and make love to my fiancée, something we hadn't done since before she left Chicago. Because the miscarriage occurred when Jaelynn was in the early stages of pregnancy, Dr. Seagram recommended that we wait three months before trying again. That meant we had to use condoms for a while, and although I wasn't happy about it, I didn't want to risk her getting pregnant too soon and suffering another loss. That would be devastating.

Kyree was letting me borrow his truck until I figured out what the move was with mine. We had to drop them off before going home, so by the time I let us into our apartment, we were exhausted. After we showered, we fell asleep as soon as our heads hit the pillow. Lovemaking would have to wait.

JAELYNN

A month had flown by, and I was still settling into my new life in Chicago. It was finally spring, but you couldn't tell that to Mother Nature. I'd never been in a snowstorm in April, but I couldn't say that now. Winter was truly nine months out of the year in this city. I'd never been so happy that I worked from home.

Unfortunately, I had to go outside today because Kamden had to go to small claims court, and I didn't want to miss it. He decided to sue Vida for the damage she caused to his car, instead of pressing charges. I actually agreed with him because, although I wanted her to be punished, when he told me that she could do one to three years in prison, I didn't push him to press charges. She was wrong, but I didn't want him to be the reason another Black woman ended up in the system. Hell, if Kamden broke up with me, I might be on the same shit that Vida was on.

"You almost ready?" Kamden said as he peeked in the bathroom.

"Give me three minutes."

"You said that ten minutes ago. I'm about to go warm up the

car. If you don't have your fine ass in the passenger seat in five minutes, I'm leaving." He tapped my ass and disappeared.

I proceeded to put my massive amount of curls into a bun. It took more than the five minutes Kamden gave me to be outside, but if he left me, he would have hell to pay.

By the time I'd got outside, he had pulled up in front of the building. When he saw me, he got out and helped me to the car. He did this all the time, but today, the sidewalk was slick, and I probably would have busted my ass. Once we were both in the car, he turned to look at me.

"You're lucky I love your ass, Jae. That was more than ten minutes."

"I'm sorry, babe. You know how hard it is to tame my hair. I'm thinking about cutting it."

"As much as I enjoy pulling on it when I hit it from the back, do what makes you happy," he told me.

"Really? You wouldn't be upset if I chopped it all off."

He shrugged his shoulders. "Why would I be upset? I love you, not your hair. I wouldn't care if you cut it into a fade and dyed it purple."

I laughed. "Yeah, okay. Let my ass come home with a purple fade. You would have a fit."

"Not at all. Try me."

"The only reason you saying that shit is because you know I'm not gon' do it. Anyway... I wanted to talk to you about something."

"I'm listening."

"Your twenty-eighth birthday is coming up, and it's your golden birthday."

"That it is."

"I wanna do something for you, but—"

"You know what I want?" He interrupted.

"What?"

"To marry you."

I lifted my hand and waved my engagement ring in his face. "We're engaged. The next logical step would be getting married."

"I know. With everything that's happened, I didn't want to pressure you to pick a date. But if you're asking me what I want for my birthday, I'm telling you that I want to marry you."

"You want to get married on your birthday?"

"There's nothing I want more."

I stared at his profile as he continued to take us to our destination. *Could I pull together a wedding in a little over two months?*

"What are you over there thinking so hard about?"

"If I can plan a wedding in less than three months."

He found a parking spot and parallel parked. Before he got out, he turned to face me.

"If I told you that I wanted to marry you next week, I think you would be able to pull off a grand affair. Between your sisters, our mothers, and Ms. Delilah, there's plenty of time."

"But we still have to move into our house—"

"Oh, you mean the house you won't decide on?"

"You know what? We should go before we're late."

I put my hand on the door and was about to open it.

"Jaelynn Michaela Waters!" he barked with authority.

I removed my hand and sat back in the seat to wait for him to open my door. He helped me out and held my hand as we approached the courthouse.

"We're going to look at three more houses when we leave here, Jae."

"I know."

"These are *nice* houses. You've looked at them a hundred times online. You said these are your final three."

"I know, Kam."

"I'm just reminding you. You gotta decide."

"I will, babe. Today is the day."

He looked at me as if he didn't believe me, then leaned down to give me a kiss before we went through the courthouse security.

"ARE you sure you never saw any signs of crazy when you were dating her?"

"First of all, our relationship wasn't that deep. But no, I never did."

"It was deep enough for you to bring her to Belize and Seattle. Don't try to downplay it now."

"I ain't downplaying shit. You heard for yourself in the courtroom that she paid for her own tickets to and from Belize, and her last-minute return ticket back from Seattle to Chicago."

Kamden was suing Vida for the costs to replace all the windows and tires, the tow, and the cleaning and detailing of the truck. She countersued for the cost of round trip tickets to Belize and the return ticket to Chicago from Seattle. The judge made him pay for the latter.

"I can't believe the judge made you pay for her ticket back to Chicago."

"I offered to do that in the first place, but she declined." He shrugged his shoulders. "It's cool, though. I'm just glad that shit is over with. I'm ready to move on from it, and I hope she learned her lesson. If she does something else crazy, I'm pressing charges against her ass."

"Damn right, you are!" I agreed.

"Enough about that. You ready to pick our new home?"

"Don't pressure me, babe. But yeah, I'm ready."

KAMDEN

Things were finally looking up. The first few months of us officially being together, Jaelynn and I had a few obstacles. I was grateful that we sought therapy, were in constant prayer, and kept the lines of communication open. A few weeks ago, I realized that it had been several days since Jaelynn had experienced a nightmare. When I brought it up to her, she actually cried. Thinking back to the conversation almost made me tear up.

We had just finished eating dinner and were sitting in the living room watching TV. It was getting late, and we would be heading to bed soon. For some reason, it dawned on me that Jaelynn hadn't been waking up in the middle of the night.

"Baby girl, how do you feel?" I asked.

She looked at me strangely for the random question.

"I feel fine."

"Do you feel extra rested? Like you've been getting a full night's rest?"

She looked to be thinking about it before she replied, "I do, actually. The past week or so, I haven't been as tired throughout the day."

"You don't even realize it, do you?" I asked her.

"Realize what?"

"You haven't had a nightmare in over a week."

"Oh my God, babe. I didn't even..." Then the tears started.

"Jae, why are you crying?"

She crawled onto my lap and straddled me before burying her face in my neck.

"Jae, what's wrong, baby girl?"

Through her tears, she cried, *"I thought the nightmares would be with me forever."*

"You just needed time. That's all."

"I needed you, babe. You don't know how much your love and support has healed me. All those nights you held me in your arms and consoled me. You were so patient with me, and... I just love you so much."

"I love you, too, Jae. I'll always be here for you. Nothing but death can keep me from it, and even then, my spirit will keep you safe and whole."

"Kam!" Jae shouted.

"Damn, Jae! Why you yelling?"

"Because I've called your name four times. Let's go."

"Oh, now you wanna rush me after I been waiting for your ass for thirty minutes."

"Be quiet and let's go sign this paperwork. I'm ready to get the keys."

After much back-and-forth, we were finally closing on our new home. I never thought this day would come, because Jaelynn had to be the most indecisive woman in the world. We made it to Vic's office about thirty-five minutes later. After about forty-five minutes of signing our lives away, we got the keys and went straight to the house.

I couldn't believe that we ended up buying the house right next door to Kyree and Braelynn. We hadn't told anyone that bit of information yet. When we got there, we went inside and stood at the front door for a minute, taking it all in.

"Do you still like it?" I asked Jaelynn.

"I love it. Let's walk through."

She grabbed my hand and pulled me along. I loved seeing her excitement, and it was definitely contagious. The house was made similar to Kyree's. It had four bedrooms, two bathrooms, a family room, formal living room and dining room, and a huge kitchen. The basement wasn't as big as I would have liked, and it was unfinished. I already had some ideas for what I wanted to do with it at some point. There were hardwood floors throughout, which Jaelynn loved but I didn't care for. I was thinking about the long-term maintenance of the floors, along with how our future children would get around.

We ended up back in the kitchen, and I pushed her against the counter. Standing in front of her, I trapped her by putting my arms on either side of her body. The smile she wore was doing something to a nigga.

"I love when your smile reaches your eyes. It lets me know that you're genuinely happy and I'm doing my job."

"I am so happy, babe."

"I am too. You know what would make me happier?"

"What's that?"

"The day you become Mrs. Kamden Isaac Ross."

"Soon you'll have your wish."

I picked her up and sat her on the counter. She opened her legs, allowing me to stand between them, and I leaned forward to kiss her lips. What I thought would be a few pecks, turned into our tongues wrestling for control. She wrapped her legs around my waist, urging me closer. My dick was harder than a muthafucka, and I wanted to be inside of her so damn bad.

It seemed as if Jaelynn and I were on the same page. Her hands went to unfasten my belt, then my slacks, and I didn't stop her. When she reached inside my boxer briefs and groped my dick, I remembered something important.

"Shit, Jae," I mumbled against her mouth. "I don't have any rubbers on me."

"Okay," she said but continued to kiss me while she massaged my manhood.

"Jae," I murmured, not wanting to stop anything that we were doing but trying my damnedest to be the responsible one.

She kept her hand on my dick but pulled her mouth away from mine. Looking at me with pleading eyes, she said, "Babe, it's been two and a half months. I think we're good."

Since the first time we made love after the miscarriage, Jaelynn did not want me to wrap up. For the past two and a half months, my strength has been tested more than ever before because Lord knows I wanted to slide up in her raw and fill her with my seeds. I couldn't take that chance, though. I wanted her to have enough time to heal before I impregnated her again.

"You sure?" I asked, knowing the decision had already been made.

"I'm positive," she replied, pushing my slacks and underwear over my ass, which freed my dick completely.

Today, Jaelynn was wearing a long, flowy, denim skirt. I pushed it up around her waist and slid her panties to the side.

"I love you so fuckin' much, baby girl," I declared as I pushed my way into her folds.

"Mmm," she moaned. "I love you."

She tightened her legs around my waist as I gripped the sides of hers. It felt so good to be inside her with nothing between us that I had a feeling my nut would come quick. Her arms went around my neck, and I buried my face in hers, inhaling her scent before letting my tongue glide across her soft skin.

"Damn, Jae!" I began to feel the familiar vibrating in my stomach and tried to think about something else because I wasn't ready to cum.

"Shit, Kam. I missed this raw dick, baby. Go deeper."

Aww, damn!

"You wanna feel this shit in your chest, Jae?"

She moaned in my ear, sending chills through my body. My hands went to her tiny, round ass, and I lifted her off the counter, then walked her to the nearest wall. With her back against it, I put my arms underneath her thighs, giving me the perfect angle to hit her deep.

"Uhhh!"

"Is this what you want? Is this deep enough, baby girl?"

"Mmmmmm," was all she said.

I deep stroked that pussy until her walls began to constrict around my dick. I prayed that she would climax soon because my shit was about to blow in five, four, three, two—

"Kam, I'm cummin'! Shit, I'm cummin'! Oh—my-fuckin'—God, I'm cummin'!" she screamed.

I growled into her neck as our fluids released and combined, making one, hot, sticky mess.

JAELYNN

*I*t was move-in day, and I was so excited. After our closing two weeks ago, Kamden wanted to get a few minor things done to the house before we moved in. Once his little projects were complete, we began taking things over that could fit in my car and his truck.

When Braelynn and Kyree found out that we'd bought the house next door to them, they were both excited. Kolby and Myla only lived a few blocks over, so I thought it was great that we were all together again.

It was finally starting to feel like spring with the temperature in the high sixties. That was comparable to how it was in Seattle during the month of May, so I couldn't complain. I stood outside of our house, waiting for the moving truck, and my phone vibrated in my back pocket. When I saw it was Myles, I answered.

"Hey, big bro!"

"Wassup, baby sis. You busy?"

"At the moment, I'm waiting for the moving truck to get here. Kam and I are moving into our house today."

"Oh shit! That's right. I guess that's why he didn't answer his phone. I just found out some shit that I think y'all should know."

For some reason, I got nervous. "Really? What's that?"

"I'm gonna send you the link to the article, and we can talk more about it when I touch down for the wedding festivities."

"Okay."

"Tell Kam I'll hit him up later. Look for the link."

He ended the call, and I held my phone in my hand as I waited for the link to come through. When it did, I clicked it, and seconds later, an article came up. As I read the article, I was in disbelief. This couldn't have ended any better than this. For a moment, I felt guilty about the joy I was experiencing, but that feeling didn't last long. The Lord would have to forgive me.

The article was about the deaths of Drake and Drew Michaels. It read like something on one of those shows on the ID channel. It said that there had been a deep-seated sibling rivalry between the brothers that dated back to the death of their parents, several years ago. The two tried to keep their dislike for each other under wraps, but it had recently come to a head, which resulted in Drew murdering his older brother, in cold blood, then setting him and his car on fire.

It went on to say that Drew had been questioned in regard to his brother's death but had an alibi. Drew later attacked Drake's former girlfriend, Jaelynn Waters, in front of her home. She shot him in self-defense, and he died while in surgery. When the police searched Drew's apartment, they found evidence that connected him to his brother's death.

Well, damn! That's an interesting turn of events.

If I didn't know most of this backstory, I would have definitely believed every word of the article. Myles and his crew were some fucking criminal geniuses. That was for damn sure.

I went back inside and kept myself busy until Kamden and the movers arrived. When the truck got here, Kyree, Kolby, Mr. Isaac,

Vic, and a few of Kamden's cousins pulled up behind it. I was grateful for all the help.

"Baby girl, why don't you go over to Kolby's place with the girls and the twins? We got it from here."

"Why? How will you know where everything goes?"

"Because you've told me a hundred times where you want everything. Go hang with your sisters. Don't you have some wedding stuff to talk about? I'll call when we're done."

We did need to discuss a few details about the wedding.

"Are you sure? I don't mind helping, babe."

"We got this." He kissed my forehead, nose, then lips, and sent me on my way.

It took me under two minutes to get to Myla's house. When I got out of my car and approached the house, I could hear the twins laughing in the backyard. I walked around to the side of the house and yelled through the tall, wooden fence.

"One of y'all heffas come open the gate."

Seconds later, Braelynn and her belly pushed the gate open. She was about six and a half months and adorable as hell. Recently, they'd found out that they were having a boy. We were all excited, but Ms. Stella gave them some grief when she found out. She wasn't satisfied with just one granddaughter and told Kamden and me that we'd better give her another girl.

"Hey, sis! How's my nephew doing?" I rubbed her belly, then gave her a hug.

"Aside from pressing on my bladder, he's fine."

"Let my nephew be," I fussed as I closed and locked the gate, then followed her into the yard.

Myla was pushing the twins on the swing set they had built last summer. The sound of their giggles filled me with so much joy. You couldn't tell those babies that there was anything better in this world than their mommy pushing them on that swing.

"Hey, Jae," Myla said, taking a quick break to give me a hug.

"Hey, My. How's Titi's babies?" I said to the twins.

They both mumbled something, but all I could understand was, "Titi."

"What are you doing here?" Braelynn asked.

"Kam made me come. Apparently, they don't need my help. Ain't no telling what my house is gonna look like when all those men unload my furniture."

"You better pray Kam follows your instructions," Myla offered.

"He claims he knows how I want everything. I'm gon' be pissed if it's not right."

"Well, think of it this way, all the hard stuff will be done."

"I suppose. We need to talk about the wedding. I have an idea I wanna run by y'all."

"We've been out here long enough. Let's go inside. The twins should be ready for their nap," Myla said.

About thirty minutes later, the twins were napping, and we were chilling in the family room. Myla and I were drinking a glass of wine while Braelynn sipped some water.

"I'm hating on y'all asses right now. I feel like y'all should be drinking water, too."

"Hell, I probably should be drinking water. My period late as fuck, but I'm in denial," Myla admitted.

Braelynn and I gasped.

"Are you for real, My?" I asked.

"Hell yeah! I knew that nigga was gon' get my ass pregnant again sooner or later."

"Well, put that damn wine down," Braelynn demanded.

Myla rolled her eyes and downed that shit. I couldn't do nothing but laugh.

"Kam and I started having sex again without a condom a couple of weeks ago. I guess there's a slight possibility that I'm pregnant, too."

"Oh, shit! I hope you are. The three of us can be pregnant together. That would be so dope," Myla said with excitement.

"My period isn't due for a couple of weeks. I'm not gonna get my hopes up, and I'm drinking this damn wine. Sorry, sis."

Braelynn threw a pillow at me, thankfully missing my glass of wine. After taking a few sips, I thought about the article that Myles had sent me.

"Hold up! I almost forgot about this shit. Myles sent me an article about Drake and Drew."

"Why?"

"What did it say?"

"It's crazy. The whole damn thing sounds like one of those crime stories on TV."

I went on to summarize the article for them. They were in utter shock just like I was.

"Is that even close to the truth?" Braelynn asked.

"Listen, all I'm gon' say is Myles and his damn crew..." I shook my head. "I know they set all this shit up to look like Drew killed Drake. I don't know if the brothers had some kind of rivalry against each other, but Drew did seem like he was jealous of Drake sometimes."

"Wow! That shit is crazy," Myla said in disbelief.

"As hell!" I agreed. "But I don't care. Both them niggas dead, and I don't feel bad about it at all. Not to mention, the case is closed, and it won't lead back to Kamden or Myles."

"True." They agreed.

"Okay, enough about that shit. Here's my idea for the wedding. I have a confession to make."

"What?" they chimed.

"I was supposed to put a down payment on that space we looked at, but I forgot."

"Damn, Jae," came from Myla.

"I know, and when I remembered, it was booked. I was upset, but honestly, I wasn't completely sold on that place. Anyway, here's my idea. What do y'all think about doing it outside? We could use our backyards." I pointed at Braelynn.

They were both quiet for a minute or so before Myla said, "I think that's a great idea. The weather should be decent, and with both yards, there would be plenty of room."

"We could rent a tent or two, and it's not like we'll have a lot of guests." I added.

"That's a great idea, Jae." Braelynn agreed. "Let's look online and see about renting a tent, some chairs, and tables. There's still a lot we need to do, and we're still cutting it close."

"How about I reach out to Erica of Evolving Diva Inc. Events? She did a great job with our baby shower and the twins' party," Myla suggested.

"Oh my God! Could you?"

Myla grabbed her phone and made the call. I prayed she didn't curse us out for such short notice. She would only have six weeks to work her magic. Myla put her phone on speaker, and I told Erica the details. She said she's planned weddings in half the time, so it wouldn't be a problem. I was so relieved and wished Myla had suggested her sooner. *Things were truly looking up!*

KAMDEN

I walked into our family room to find Jaelynn taking a nap on the couch. I suspected that she might be pregnant but didn't want to bring it up. We'd been settled into our new home for a few weeks. Between unpacking, working, and planning our wedding, she could just be tired.

Kneeling on the floor next to the couch, I leaned in and kissed the exposed area of Jaelynn's neck. She stirred, putting one of her hands on the top of my head. I went from a simple kiss to licking and sucking her neck until she moaned.

"Kaamm, I'm trying to take a nap."

"I'm gon' put you right back to sleep. I want some pussy."

I kept kissing, licking, and sucking on her neck, while positioning my body on top of hers. She opened her legs, allowing me to settle in the perfect position with my dick right on her center. She was wearing a loose-fitting tank top and a pair of thin ass pajama shorts with no panties underneath. All I had on was a pair of basketball shorts, sans underwear. Needless to say, when we started grinding against each other, that shit was feeling right.

The precum began to seep from the head of my dick, wetting

up the front of my shorts. All this friction had to stop before I came prematurely. I slid my body down, taking Jaelynn's shorts with me. She lifted up, assisting me with removing them from her body, and I tossed them on the floor. With her legs on my shoulders, my tongue went deep-sea diving in her pussy.

"Ahh, damn," Jaelynn crooned.

It only took a few minutes of licking, sucking, and applying pressure to the right place, and Jaelynn was wetting up my whole damn face. I didn't let up, though. I wanted her to cum one more time before I blessed her with the stiffness between my legs.

"Kam, please," she begged when I relentlessly flicked my tongue through her crevices.

She could beg all she wanted. I wasn't letting up until she drowned my ass. When her hands pressed the back of my head and she lifted her pelvic area up toward my face, I knew she was about to give me exactly what I wanted.

"Ahhhhh," she screamed.

I caught every ounce of liquid that leaked from her juicy pussy. Getting on my knees, I slipped out of my shorts and threw them on the floor. Jaelynn looked at me with her eyes low and a sexy ass smile. My hand went to my dick, and I gave it a few strokes. She reached for it, and I swatted her hand away.

"You want this dick, baby girl?"

She nodded.

"I thought you wanted to take a nap."

"Kam, stop playing."

"Tell me you want the dick."

"Babe, I want the dick, and I want it right fuckin' now."

I stopped stroking but kept my hand on my dick. Using my free hand for leverage, I slid right into her awaiting oasis.

"Ahh, fuck!"

Leaning down, I covered her mouth with mine, pushing my tongue inside, sharing her sweet nectar with her. Jaelynn's legs clamped around my waist, and she used the heels of her feet to push me deeper. Taking the cue from her, I gave her repeated deep strokes while we French kissed like two reunited lovers. When she began to match my strokes, I knew her peak was near.

She tore her mouth away from mine and screamed, "Kamdeeeennnn! I'm cummin'!"

As she reached her point of ecstasy, her pussy milked me into reaching mine. After that nut, it was definitely nap time.

"CAN YOU BELIEVE IT, babe? We're pregnant!"

Another few weeks had past, and I couldn't take it anymore. I went to a pharmacy and picked up a few home pregnancy tests. When I got home, Jaelynn willingly took all of them. Currently, I was sitting on the edge of our jacuzzi tub in my underwear, holding three tests that all read *positive* in my hand while Jaelynn stood naked in front of the sink. This moment seemed surreal because it was a first for us. The way shit went down before... I shook off the thought. Right now, I was thankful for this experience.

"Yeah, we're pregnant," was my reply. I still hadn't taken my eyes off the tests.

"Kam, babe, are you okay?"

She walked toward me and stood in front of me. Her stomach was right in front of my face. I put the tests on the edge of the jacuzzi and pulled her closer, resting my head on her stomach.

"I'm more than okay. You just made me the happiest man in the world."

I planted soft, lingering kisses all over her stomach, while I squeezed her ass. My dick stiffened, and I knew we were gonna be late to our bachelor and bachelorette parties. I stood and pushed off my boxers.

"Babe, we don't have time—"

Jaelynn tried to protest, but I shut her up with a kiss while backing her up to the sink. When her butt hit the edge, I turned her around and bent her over. Before she could brace herself, I slid into her wetness and released a satisfied growl.

"I love this fuckin' pussy, Jae."

"I love this dick more."

"Naw, baby girl. That's impossible," I told her as I deep stroked her juicy pussy.

She held onto the sink as best she could as I pounded her from the back. Reaching in front of her, I found her spot with my index and middle finger and applied just the right amount of pressure, while moving my fingers in a circular motion.

"Ssss," she hissed. "It feels so good."

"Cum on this dick then, baby girl. Wet it up," I commanded.

As always, her pussy responded and clutched around my dick, forcing me to fill her to the rim.

"Arrggh," I groaned against her back.

We didn't move for a good minute, her laying on the sink and me on her back. When I stood and slowly pulled myself from my haven, I immediately felt her absence. Jaelynn remained bent over the counter of the sink while I started the shower. Once the water was warm enough, I tapped Jaelynn on the ass.

"Come on. We gon' be late to our own shit," I urged.

"If I shower with you, we might not make it at all. I'll go to the guest bathroom."

"Girl, if you don't bring your ass on."

I pulled her toward the shower, and she got in first. She was exactly right, though. After another session in the shower, I damn near wanted to cancel everything. Somehow, we managed to make it out the door.

JAELYNN

*I*t was a shame that we were late getting to Braelynn and Kyree's house, considering they lived right next door. We didn't care, though. Kamden and I were on cloud nine about the baby and the fact that we were getting married in two weeks.

We decided not to tell anyone about the baby until the reception. I wasn't sure how I was going to keep it from my sisters, especially since we'd already talked about the possibility. Myla had told the family that she was expecting two weeks ago, and I know, if no one else, she and Braelynn were expecting to hear something from me soon.

Kamden and I chose tonight to have our bachelor and bachelorette parties because next week was our coed wedding shower. We walked into our siblings' house, and all eyes were on us.

"What?" I said, defensively.

"Nothing." Braelynn began. "But since you walked in looking thoroughly fucked, I know why y'all are late."

"Shut up with yo' pregnant ass," I tossed back with a laugh.

"Y'all straight, bruh. I know exactly how it is," Kyree commented as he approached Kamden to give him some dap.

"We've been waiting a while, though." Myla added with raised eyebrows.

"Baby, we just got here two minutes ago for the same reason. When that pregnant pussy takes a nigga hostage, it's a done deal." Kolby added.

"You ain't lying." Kamden agreed.

Suddenly, the room got quiet, and four pairs of eyes were on us again.

"Hold the fuck up! Are you saying what we think you're saying?" Kyree questioned.

I looked up at Kamden and shrugged my shoulders. He pulled me in front of him and wrapped his arms around me, then kissed my cheek.

"We're pregnant!" we both said.

Our siblings shouted with excitement and wrapped us in a group hug. Keeping it from them lasted all of three minutes. They all gave their congratulations, and we finally left to get our night of partying started. The guys hopped in Kyree's truck while we took Kolby's with Myla behind the wheel.

Our significant others thought we were having dinner with some of their female cousins and a few models that we still talked to from our fashion show, which was true. However, once we finished eating, we were headed to the strip club. If they knew that, they would have shut that shit down immediately. We didn't even ask their plans, because we didn't want to divulge ours. Them going to a strip club wasn't an issue for us, so we let them be great.

We reserved a section of tables at a restaurant called The Delta, which was on the north side of Chicago. I'd heard a lot of great things about it, and I couldn't wait to try it. Since we were running late, everyone was waiting for us. In total, there were only ten of us.

I made sure to tell them not to mention me being pregnant. Thankfully, at the restaurant, no one was drinking liquor, and I didn't have to explain to anyone why I wasn't. Dinner was amazing, and I couldn't wait to go back there with my husband.

When we arrived at the strip club, I was giddy. I'd never been to one before because I had no desire to see a bunch of no-rhythm-having white men take off their clothes. But when Kamden's cousin, Jameka, told me about Black Diamond, I was all in. None of them would be as fine as my babe, but I was down for being entertained.

"Me and this big ass belly need to be off in the cut. I don't want these niggas touching my stomach," Braelynn said.

"You know, Kyree is going to kill you if he finds out you got his baby up in this strip club," I told her.

"He sure is." Myla agreed.

She looked at us with a frown. "Umm, y'all are pregnant, too. What the hell you think Kolby and Kam are gonna do? We gon' all be in trouble together."

Myla and I looked at each other and shrugged our shoulders with a laugh. We followed our group to the area where we were being seated, which was right up front. I had on a tiara and a sash that read *Mrs. Ross-to-be,* and they sat me right in the middle of our group. I was so happy and just wanted to celebrate and have a good time.

As soon as the show started, I was out of my seat as "Grind on Me" by Pretty Ricky blasted through the speakers. The men on the stage were sexy as hell—all different flavors of chocolate with their muscles glistening under the lights. I had my singles ready and was acting a plum fool, waving them in the air and catcalling the niggas. At one point, the strippers came to our area and surrounded me. While they did their sexy dances, I rubbed their bodies and put some singles in their bikini thongs.

"This next one coming out is fine as hell. Here, take these singles," Jameka offered.

She's clearly a regular!

All of Kamden's female cousins that we'd met over the past couple of years were cool as hell. Jameka was the wildest one, and we could always count on her when it was time to kick it. I took the singles as another group of strippers graced the stage. They came out to "Pony" by Ginuwine, and the place went crazy, me included.

When the main attraction of that group, made his sexy ass way toward me, somebody pushed me into the aisle, and *baby*, me and Mr. Stripper Man start putting on a show. He did a slow grind to the beat of the song against my pelvic area, then suddenly, picked me up, and my legs went around his waist. He continued to gyrate as he held me up, and not even thirty seconds later, my ass was being snatched away from him.

It only took me five seconds to realize what was happening. I smelled his cologne as he tossed me over his shoulder and marched right on out of the door of the club.

Uh oh! I think I'm in trouble.

KAMDEN

*M*y brothers and I, along with a few of my male cousins, met up at the hotel suite that Myles had reserved. Kyree and Kolby were in on all the planning but wouldn't tell me anything. I told them that I wasn't really feeling going to a strip club, so they decided to have the strippers come to the suite.

The niggas my female cousins were dating were invited as well, so there was a decent-sized group of us. I was happy about that because I didn't want to be the center of attention.

My brothers and soon-to-be brother-in-law hooked it up for a nigga, though. There was plenty of food, drinks, and weed to go around, and I indulged in it all. While we waited for the strippers to arrive, some of us sat around talking shit, some played spades, and some played dominoes.

Once the strippers arrived, shit got wild. There were three of them, and they were definitely masters at their craft. At some point, I'd gotten a lap dance from all three of them, and I couldn't wait to get home to Jaelynn. I was horny as fuck.

The strippers took a little break, and I took out my phone and went to my Instagram. I saw that my cousin Jameka had posted a new story, and when I opened it, I was pretty sure steam was coming out of my ears.

"What the fuck!" I yelled, loud enough to be heard over the music.

Kolby took my phone, and his face immediately went into a frown.

"What the fuck y'all niggas looking at?" Myles asked.

"My damn wife getting groped by some buff ass stripper!" Kolby spat.

Myles took my phone to see what he was talking about, and Kyree looked over his shoulder.

"Didn't they say they were going out to eat? I know damn well my seven-and-a-half-month pregnant wife is not at no damn strip club," Kyree fumed.

Kolby had his phone out, pressing shit, and said, "Their asses are at Black Diamond. Let's go."

Myles and my cousins were talking shit and cracking up at our ass as we hightailed it outta there. When my cousins' boyfriends found out where we were headed, they fell in line, too. Myles and my male cousins stayed in the suite and continued to kick it.

It took us twenty minutes to get to the club. There were six of us, and we probably looked strange entering a club with male strippers. I wasn't sure how common that was, because I'd never visited one. The woman at the door took our money as she looked at us with wide, surprised eyes. Security patted us down but, thankfully, didn't ask any questions.

When we got inside, it wasn't hard to spot Jaelynn. Her ass was being held by one of the fuck ass strippers, with her legs wrapped around his waist, looking like she was having the time of her life. I marched my ass up to her and snatched her away from the nigga. She didn't even see me coming and neither did any of the other ladies in the group. They were too busy drooling over these niggas.

I tossed her little ass over my shoulder and headed right back out the door. We paid the valet to hold the truck in front. I opened the back door and put her inside. She moved to the other side, and I slid in next to her. I slammed the door, and as much as I wanted to go off, I ain't say shit. When she looked like she wanted to open her mouth, I glared at her, and she decided against it.

Not even a minute later, Kyree opened the passenger side door and helped Braelynn get inside. I caught the look that Braelynn and Jaelynn exchanged, but neither of them said a word. When Kyree walked across the front of the car, I could tell he was pissed. I assumed Myla and Kolby left in his truck. The ride home was in complete silence. Not even the radio was on. Jaelynn kept her head facing the window and didn't try to talk to me again.

When we pulled into Kolby's driveway, he stopped to let us out before he pulled into the garage. I hopped out, and Jaelynn got out right behind me. After letting us into our house, I went to the kitchen and tossed my keys on the counter, then turned and leaned against it. I looked at Jaelynn and got heated all over again.

"What the fuck was that, Jae? I thought y'all were going out to dinner. You ain't say shit about a strip club."

"Kamden—"

"Don't *Kamden* me. What the hell were you doing?"

"I was just having fun! Why are you making a big deal about it?"

"Because it's a big deal. You're about to be my wife and you're carrying my child. That ain't the kinda shit I wanna see."

"You weren't supposed to see it," she almost whispered.

"The fuck you mean? Jameka's ass got it posted all over her damn Instagram story. How the fuck was I not supposed to see it?"

"I mean, it wasn't meant for you to see. I was just having fun, and you need to calm down. You act like you've never had a lap dance."

"That's different."

"How is that different Kamden?"

"'Cause that's what niggas do. We get lap dances."

"Are you kidding me right now?" She folded her arms across her chest.

"I'm serious as hell. This shit is different."

"Y'all didn't go to a strip club tonight?"

"Nope," I stated proudly.

She took out her phone and pressed some buttons. I heard music and a bunch of male voices as she stared at the screen. I knew exactly what she was looking at.

"Where is this?" She moved closer so I could see her phone as she held it up.

I should have made everyone at my party put away their phones. *How the hell am I gon' justify being mad at Jaelynn when she has video evidence of me getting a lap dance from not one, not two, but three damn strippers?*

"Myles got a suite because I didn't want to go to a strip club."

"Which means you had your own personal strippers! I can't believe you, Kamden. You got a lot of nerve!"

"At least you didn't have to come snatch some woman off my lap like I had to come snatch your ass off some niggas dick!"

"First of all, I wasn't on nobody's damn dick. I was around his waist, and I ain't feel shit. Stop exaggerating. Secondly, I would have let you finish enjoying your party."

"You mean to tell me you're not pissed about me getting a lap dance?"

"You didn't get *a* lap dance; you got *three*. And no, I'm not mad at all." She was serious, too.

"Why the fuck not?" I asked, slightly annoyed.

"Kam, what is wrong with you? You're mad that I'm not mad?"

"You should feel some type of way. What woman wants another woman grinding all on her man?"

Jaelynn pressed her hand against her forehead, then tousled her curls. She came and leaned her body against mine, putting her arms around my neck and looking up and into my eyes.

"Babe, I don't want another woman grinding all over my man.

However, if you go to a strip club occasionally and get a lap dance, I'm not gon' be fucked up about it. What I will do is fuck you real good before you go and be butt-ass naked playing with my pussy when you get home. I'm not gon' trip about it, though."

My dick got hard at the thought of walking into our bedroom to find her playing with her pussy. As I looked into her eyes, I saw nothing but love. Maybe I exaggerated a little bit, but I wasn't telling her ass that. She might think it was cool to do some shit like that again.

"I guess both of us can't be jealous as hell. Let's go shower so you can wash that nigga's scent off you and I can eat that pussy from the back."

"You so damn nasty."

"I know. After I finish eating it from the back, I'm gon' leave the room, and when I come back, I wanna see you playing in that shit. Then we'll be cool again."

She laughed, but I was serious as hell. "Boy, your ass is crazy."

I may have been crazy, but everything I said happened when we got in that bedroom.

JAELYNN

*I*t was the day that I would become Mrs. Kamden Isaac Ross. Everything was decorated beautifully in lavender, off-white, and gold, and the weather was absolutely perfect.

I stood in front of the full-length mirror in my bedroom and admired the view. No one would ever believe that I found this dress on the rack at a bridal store that was going out of business. With only minor alterations that my mother was able to do, it fit perfectly.

"I still can't believe you did it, Jae," Braelynn said.

"I love it! She looks beautiful." Myla added.

"Of course she does. But I still can't believe she did it. How do you feel?"

"Amazing," was all I said in reply.

"Okay, Jae. It's time. Your father would be so proud of you. I'm sure he's looking down on you with a smile from ear to ear."

"I know, Ma. I miss him so much, but I know he's watching over me."

We had a quick moment of silence. I was sure she was thinking about my dad, just as I was.

"Come on girls. Let's go get in position. Stella and Isaac are already there. Uncle David is waiting outside. He'll knock on the door when it's time."

My mom kissed and hugged me, being careful not to mess up my makeup or dress, then disappeared.

"Okay, sis! We'll see you on the other side."

After a hug and kiss from my matrons of honor, they were gone as well. I was alone with my thoughts as I waited for the knocks from my uncle.

Kamden and I had been through so much to get to this point. There were times when I worried that our love wasn't strong enough to endure all of the obstacles. Hell, I wondered if *I* was strong enough.

I knew we shouldn't look to others to make us whole and that we should be able to feel complete without the help of others. After being raped, I'd lost some of myself and didn't care to find it again. But Kamden's love for me healed my heart in such a way that made me want to be whole again. I was so grateful for his love and patience with me.

The knocks on the door took me out of my thoughts. Taking a deep breath and looking at my single self one last time in the full-length mirror, I was ready to become Mrs. Kamden Isaac Ross.

KAMDEN

$\mathcal{E}$veryone was in place, and I was anxiously waiting for my bride. "Heaven Sent" by Keyshia Cole began to play, and I knew that the next person to come down the aisle would be my baby girl. When she appeared, I couldn't hold back my tears, and my knees got weak. She looked so fuckin' beautiful. I felt someone's hands on my shoulders, pulling me back. When I looked to the side, I saw Kyree.

"Yo, Kam. You gotta wait here, bruh. She's coming to you."

I looked around and realized that I'd started walking down the aisle. Taking a few steps back into my position, my eyes went back to Jaelynn. My excitement was through the roof because she was seconds away from being right next to me, and we were minutes away from becoming one.

When she and Uncle David made it to the end of the aisle, they stopped, and my eyes locked on hers. The smile she wore was wide, and it reached her eyes, which made me smile even wider.

I heard the pastor say, "Who gives this woman to this man?"

Ms. Lynn stood, and she and Uncle David both said, "We do."

As soon as Uncle David left her side, I took his place and took her in my arms.

"Happy birthday, babe."

"Thank you, baby girl. You cut your hair and dyed it purple. You look so fu—so beautiful." I reached up and touched the nape of her neck, admiring her curly fade.

"You like it?"

"I love it. I love you." I cupped her face with both hands and kissed her lips.

"Whoa, young man. Slow down and let me get you married first," the pastor said.

"My bad."

Jaelynn reached up and wiped my lips before we turned to face the pastor, holding hands.

Let's get this show on the road.

EPILOGUE

Nine Months Later

JAELYNN

"Kam, can you change her diaper before I nurse her on the other side?"

"Of course, baby girl."

He took our daughter from my arms and proceeded to change her diaper. I watched him as I thought about the previous nine months. After the wedding, we honeymooned in Belize for seven days. When we returned, we settled into marital bliss. I swear, God couldn't have given me a better husband. Kamden was everything that I could have asked for in a husband.

In August, Braelynn gave birth to Kyree Isaac Ross, Jr. She

adjusted to motherhood well and had found herself pregnant again. *Yep, already.* They were expecting baby number two in September.

Myla and I ended up only being weeks apart in our pregnancy. Kolana Ivy Ross was born two weeks before her little cousin, Jaeden Michenzie Ross. With all these babies, it was a wonder that we'd been able to keep our business afloat. MyLynn's Bedroom Boutique was still flourishing, and we couldn't be more grateful.

My mother and Auntie Dee couldn't stand being away from all their babies any longer and have both moved to Chicago. I knew it would happen eventually, and we were glad to have them here.

Auntie Dee was living with Myla, for now, but had plans to get her own place soon. My mother rotated between our house and next door, although, right now, she was spending more time here because Jaeden was only a month old.

Kamden finished changing Jaeden's diaper, and she started to get fussy.

"What's wrong with daddy's girl? You still hungry? You wanna suck on your mama's titties some more?"

"Kam!"

He looked at me innocently. "What?"

"Stop talking to my baby like that."

"Well, shit. It's true. That's all her little ass does is eat, shit, and whine. Ain't that right, daddy's girl? But it's cool. Daddy loves you, and you can do and have anything you want for the rest of your life. That's right. Daddy gon' give you the world, baby girl. You and your fine ass mama."

He planted soft kisses over her chubby cheeks before handing her back to me. I loved seeing him in Daddy mode. It was so damn sexy. I loved this man with my whole heart, and I could definitely see myself giving him as many babies as he wanted.

KAMDEN

$\mathscr{I}$ always knew that loving Jaelynn would have me doing shit that could land my ass in jail. None of that shit mattered because I'd do all that shit and more all over again in a heartbeat. It took longer than I wanted to make her mine, and we had to go through some hard times to find our happiness. But as I stood in the doorway and watched Jaelynn and Jaeden peacefully asleep in the rocking chair, I knew everything we went through was worth it.

I quietly entered the room and tried to take Jaeden out of Jaelynn's arms. She held her tighter and opened her eyes.

"I'm just putting her in her crib," I told her.

I could tell she was slightly discombobulated. The first month of parenthood had been rough. I wasn't gon' even lie and say we enjoyed every minute of it. The lack of sleep was even worse than the lack of sex. I'd been doing my best to make sure Jaelynn gets as much rest as possible. No matter how much I tried to help, she was still doing most of the work.

When I took Jaeden, she balled up her little body, then stretched like she had just got home from working third shift. After kissing the top of her head, I placed her in her crib, and then she settled down and went back to sleep.

I went back to the rocking chair and scooped up my big baby bridal style and took her back to our bedroom. She was barely awake when I placed her in our bed and pulled the comforter over her. Kissing her forehead, her nose, then her lips, I was about to walk away until I heard her call my name.

"You need something, baby girl?"

"Come lay with me."

I walked around to the other side of the bed and took off my shirt and basketball shorts, leaving me in my boxers. When I slid in next to her, she turned around to face me.

"You're such a good husband and father, Kam. I appreciate you so much. Your love penetrated the guard I had up and healed my heart in ways I didn't think was possible. Thank you, babe."

"Jae, I love you more now than I did yesterday and less than I will tomorrow. My life would be nothing without you, and I would do anything to keep you safe and happy."

After exchanging a few kisses, we dozed off, only to be awakened what seemed like minutes later by the little being that our love created.

THE END

AFTERWORD

Dear Readers

Thank you pushing me to write Kamden and Jaelynn's story. I hope you enjoyed. The babies of this bunch put me through it, but I'm glad I pushed through and let their voices be heard. If you could please leave a review on Amazon and/or Goodreads, I would greatly appreciate it. Until next time.

Kay Shanee

CONNECT WITH KAY SHANEE

You can find me at all of the following:

Reading Group: Kay Shanee's Reading Korner – After Dark
Facebook page: Author Kay Shanee
Instagram: @AuthorKayShanee
Goodreads: Kay Shanee
Subscribe to my mailing list: Subscribe to Kay Shanee
Website at www.AuthorKayShanee.com

OTHER BOOKS BY KAY SHANEE

Love Hate and Everything in Between

Love Doesn't Hurt

Love Unconventional

I'd Rather Be With You

Can't Resist This Complicated Love

Love's Sweet Serenade

The Love I Deserve

Loving Him Through The Storm

Since the Day We Met

COMPLETED SERIES
UNTIL THE WHEELS FALL OFF

Until the Wheels Fall Off...Again

Could This Be Love ~ Part 1

Could This Be Love ~Part 2

CPSIA information can be obtained
at www.ICGtesting.com
Printed in the USA
LVHW021544061120
670969LV00010B/935